A Sherlock Holmes and the Charlie Chaplin Affair

Val Andrews

First published in 2020 by
The Irregular Special Press
for Baker Street Studios Ltd
Endeavour House
170 Woodland Road, Sawston
Cambridge, CB22 3DX, UK

Overall © Baker Street Studios Ltd, 2020

All rights reserved

No parts of this publication may be reproduced, stored in retrieval systems or transmitted in any form or by any means, electronic, mechanical, photocopying, recording or otherwise, except brief extracts for the purposes of review, without prior permission of the publishers.

Any paperback edition of this book, whether published simultaneously with, or subsequent to, the case bound edition, is sold subject to the condition that it shall not by way of trade, be lent, resold, hired out or otherwise disposed of without the publisher's consent, in any form of binding or cover other than that in which it was published.

This is a work of fiction. Names, characters, businesses, places, events and incidents are either the products of the author's imagination or used in a fictitious manner. Any resemblance to actual persons, living or dead, or actual events is purely coincidental.

ISBN: 978-1-901091-71-7

Cover Illustration: Public domain image of Charlie Chaplin in his 'Tramp' persona. *The Tramp* was released on 11th April 1915 through Essanay Studios.

Typeset in 8/11/20pt Palatino

About the Author

During his life Val Andrews wrote over thirty new Sherlock Holmes adventures and was always at his best when writing about the world of entertainment, in which he worked as a writer and performer for fifty years. From a theatrical background, he was a professional vaudeville artiste, ventriloquist, magician and scriptwriter to Tommy Cooper, Benny Hill and other comedy legends of stage and television. He could even count among his friends the likes of Orson Welles.

Val Andrews was born in Hove near Brighton on the 15th February 1926 only a few hours after Valentine's Day and hence his Christian name. He was the son of an architect and indeed it was his father who introduced him to magic, a fascination that was to last a lifetime and was to result in many biographies on the great magicians and numerous writings on magic in general.

He died from a heart attack on the 12th October 2006 and will be missed but at least his name will live on through his books that continue to thrill old and new murder mystery enthusiasts alike.

Sherlock Holmes and the Charlie Chaplin Mystery is the last Val Andrews book to be published, and was also his favourite to write and research. As ever it mixes fact with fiction, and introduces the reader to the world of vaudeville and film that was so familiar to him.

By The Same Author

Sherlock Holmes and the Baker Street Dozen
Sherlock Holmes and the Circus of Fear
Sherlock Holmes and the Egyptian Hall Adventure
Sherlock Holmes and the Greyfriars School Mystery
Sherlock Holmes and the Hilldrop Crescent Mystery
Sherlock Holmes and the Holborn Emporium
Sherlock Holmes and the Houdini Birthright
Sherlock Holmes and the Long Acre Vampire
Sherlock Holmes and the Man Who Lost Himself
Sherlock Holmes and the Sandringham House Mystery
Sherlock Holmes and the Secret Seven
Sherlock Holmes and the Theatre of Death
Sherlock Holmes and the Tomb of Terror
Sherlock Holmes and the Yule-tide Mystery
Sherlock Holmes at the Varieties
Sherlock Holmes on the Western Front
Sherlock Holmes: The Ghost of Baker Street
The Torment of Sherlock Holmes

The following novel combines fact intertwined with fictional elements from the fertile imagination of Val Andrews. At the heart of the story is Hannah Chaplin who was born at 11 Camden Street, London in 1865 as Hannah Harriet Pedlingham Hill. She was the mother of Charlie Chaplin (and his two half-brothers, the actor Sydney Chaplin and the film director Wheeler Dryden), and was an actress, singer and dancer in her own right. She performed in music halls under her stage name of Lily Harley from the age of sixteen and even toured Northern America in 1890, just a year after giving birth to Charlie and at a time when her health was starting to give cause for concern.

As a result of her mental illness, most likely syphilis, she was unable to continue her career from the mid-1890s. On 29th June 1895 she was admitted to the Lambeth Infirmary with Charlie ending up in an orphanage. Her condition deteriorated with her being admitted to the Cane Hill Asylum when she was thirty-one. After her release she lived for a short while in an inexpensive room in Kennington, but was readmitted to hospital just two years later. By the time Charlie was twenty-one he had earned enough money to travel to the States where his career took off, while his mother's illness deepened further into a state of dementia.

In 1921, desperate to see his mother, Charlie had her brought to Hollywood, where she was cared for in a house in the San Fernando Valley until her death in August 1928. Charlie was at her side.

Chapter One

The Charlie Chaplin Mystery

During the period which immediately followed the Great War (1914–1918) I saw very little of my friend Mr. Sherlock Holmes. Indeed, regular readers of my accounts of his exploits will know that Holmes had retired from public life in 1904, whilst at the very peak of his brilliant career. Devoting himself to the husbandry of bees and deep contemplation he had since then refused all temptations to become involved in criminal investigation, save where the welfare of his country was at stake. Oh yes, as his closest, indeed only, friend I admit that I had been able to lure him from the Sussex Downs on one or two occasions. I had never pleaded with him by word or deed, yet he knew me well enough to realise that I would have been grossly disappointed with his lack of participation.

One of these rare episodes began in the September of 1921 when Holmes had invited me to spend a few days with him at Fowlhaven, the village near Eastbourne where his retreat was situated. On the morning following the day of my arrival we had taken a brisk walk upon the Downs. My old war wound meant that I had experienced difficulty as always in keeping up with my friend, sixty-seven winters having done little to slow him down. We had surveyed the wonderful view of the sea from a grass hill scarred with chalk diggings and then had made our way more easily, for it was all downhill, in returning to Holmes's cottage. We made our way down the chalk track which led to the back gate, and as we passed the neat row of beehives we could see clearly the bonnet of a large motor car which was standing in the lane in front of the cottage.

"Are you expecting anyone to contact you here, Watson?"

"I do not believe that a living soul knows where I am."

My friend shrugged. "Well, I am certainly not expecting anyone, yet find myself graced by the visit of a person of considerable wealth. The Mercedes is second only to the Rolls Royce in value, is it not?"

Amused by how this retired detective had kept such a finger on the pulse of topical matters, I asked, "Could it perhaps be that a motorist has lost his way and is asking directions of your housekeeper?"

He shook his head as we made a detour, changing his original plan to enter the cottage by its rear door.

He said, "You will notice that the engine is switched off and the driver is reading a novella whilst his passenger is inside, awaiting my return." Then as we followed the path which led to the front door, he added, "Our visitor is a small man in peak condition. You will notice from the imprints in the damp chalk that his feet are small and he walks lightly, almost upon his toes, like an athlete or an acrobat. I rather favour the latter, for few athletes are of petite build. But one thing puzzles me."

"What, pray?"

"The fact that one seldom encounters a wealthy acrobat, rich enough to hire, let alone own such a motor car."

I could not imagine why he did not simply enter his house and see who his visitor could be.

As if reading my mind, he said, "I need to practice the art of deduction, Watson. I seldom have the opportunity to use it these days but one dislikes the possibility of age withering one's abilities. His shoes, you will notice, are bespoke. You will have noticed the imprints of hand-stitching at the edge of the soles. Although of affluence, he is a self-made man, as yet still careful with his money. Notice that the shoes have been repaired to an extent suggesting that they had reached a stage where your average man of wealth would have discarded them."

As we went through the front door, Holmes raised a hand to silence the obviously excited housekeeper. Gently he brushed past her as we moved into the sitting room with its sheepskin rugs and the furnishings of a bygone age – the general scene rather spoiled by what I can only describe as the 'clutter of 221B Baker Street'. There upon the mahogany carver perched a rather distinguished-looking young man. I noted that he was perhaps three and thirty, short of stature and of slim build. He wore a grey jacket and tan trousers, both well-tailored, with a collar attached sports shirt, open at the neck, his throat covered by a Paisley bandana. His features were agreeable rather than handsome, and despite his comparative youth his luxuriant dark hair was flecked with grey. When he smiled, I noticed that his top teeth bordered upon prominence. I did not recognise him, but Holmes obviously did.

"Good morning, Mr. Chaplin. I am Sherlock Holmes and this is my friend and erstwhile colleague, Dr. John Watson."

I could see that our visitor was surprised.

"Mr. Holmes, your recognition flatters me."

My friend smiled enigmatically as he said, "Oh come, sir, I may be something of a recluse, but even I have been known to visit the Kinema de Luxe in Eastbourne where I have enjoyed a number of your filmatic farces. One does not easily forget a comical genius, especially when one has met the artiste before."

Chaplin smiled engagingly. "I did not think that you would remember my portrayal of Billy the Page in the play with William Gillette."

I recalled then his cavorting as the pageboy, but had seen none of his films. Holmes led Chaplin to a more comfortable chair and said, "I congratulate you on your deserved success, Mr. Chaplin, yet I am puzzled to return from my walk to discover you in my sitting room. However, I neglect my duties as a host. Watson, be so good as to request Mrs. Hudson to produce a pot of coffee and some scones."

Without bothering to correct his mistake, I passed his request to Mrs. McDonald who had long given up upon chastising my friend for calling her Hudson. She was bubbling with enthusiasm as I spoke to her in the kitchen.

She said, "Doctor, I tried to inform you both that Charlie Chaplin was in the sitting room. I recognised him at once, even without his funny hat and baggy trousers. He was very pleasant to me, so polite and he has a lovely smile. But watch the china, you know how clumsy he can be."

I suppressed a guffaw, and decided to make no comment to the effect that Chaplin had perhaps been acting when she had seen him dropping dishes at the Kinema de Luxe. Indeed, I was later to be captivated with Mr. Chaplin's dainty movements as he sipped his coffee and even more so when he gave us an impromptu performance. He used two forks, two scones and the bandana from his neck: this he tucked into the collar of his shirt and impaling a scone upon each fork, he held these behind the cambric which gave the impression of feet which he moved in a dance step upon the table. His clever facial expressions added to the effect of a mannequin, rather like the living marionettes of the music hall stage. He hummed a little tune as he moved the scones in a step dance. Holmes and I applauded and my friend congratulated him.

"You really must include that delightful interlude in one of your moving picture plays."

Chaplin said, "I may well do so one day, Mr. Holmes. The idea came from a vaudeville act that was on the bill when I toured with the Fred Karno company. But come, I must not occupy too much of your time before getting to the point of my visit."

Sherlock Holmes raised an admonishing finger, saying, "Before you do so, Mr. Chaplin, you must remember that I have long forsaken my role as a private investigator. Were you about to request my services as such, I can only say that our friends at Scotland Yard may well be able to recommend one of those who have followed in my footsteps, if they are unable to assist you themselves."

The Charlie Chaplin Mystery

In retrospect, I believe that Holmes was well aware of the route that Chaplin's reply would take, even if his actual problem was unclear to him. But he made none of this clear from his manner and leant forward in his chair as if not wishing to miss any scrap of speech that Chaplin might utter.

"Mr. Holmes, although I have made my mark as a comedic film actor, I have not always been a success. Indeed, my fame is fairly recent, as indeed is the popularity of moving pictures themselves. My parents were both music hall performers: my father, Charles Chaplin senior, had a taste of stardom, short lived due to his liking for the bottle. My childhood and that of my half-brother Sydney, was marred by domestic upheavals, poverty too, as my poor dear mother tried so hard to support us, first as a performer herself, but later as a seamstress, a laundry maid and a charwoman, for her nerves would not stand up to the demands of the theatre. There were times when she was forced to sell or pawn many of our possessions and in the end she was frequently in and out of nursing homes and asylums whilst Syd and I were often sent to children's institutions. Always, somehow, we seemed ultimately to be reunited, the three of us, whilst the authorities searched, usually without success, for my errant father."

I felt slightly uncomfortable as I listened to this sad narrative and wondered where on earth it could be leading. Shifting uncomfortably in my chair, I noticed that Holmes remained impassive. Chaplin had paused, either from emotion or for effect, but quickly recommenced.

"But things changed rather for the better when first Sydney, and then I became old enough to begin to bring in a little money. We both obtained work as boy acrobatic comedians. We each had talents for song and dance and were kept busy as members of various touring troupes such as the Lancashire Lads, Casey's Court and later we both became quite prominent members of Fred Karno's touring comic sketches. Notably the Mumming Birds, which was a burlesque of an old-time music hall where I made quite a success as the drunk who interrupted the turns from the box. Karno took us several times on tour in America, and to cut all the corners, Syd and I were not able indefinitely to resist the offers made to us by makers of moving pictures. Of course, we had left Mother in the care of good friends, but on my last visit I found that she had been again confined to an asylum. My work made it impossible for me to stay for long and then came the war and this is the first time I have been able to get back to England, home and beauty. I am here now partly on business, but mainly of course to see my mother."

Holmes stabbed sharply. "But you have not seen her?"

Chaplin started. "How could you know that?"

My friend shrugged impatiently, "Oh, come, my dear Chaplin, your narrative has centred upon your maternal parent; she is obviously the main concern in your visit to me. Had you seen her you would have found her either improved in health or still with some form of senility. In the latter case you could only have, with your new-found affluence, have provided for her needs in more comfortable surroundings. If she had proved better, you would doubtless have taken her to America with you. In either case there would be no problem that would make you seek the assistance of Sherlock Holmes. Clearly you have been unable to make contact with your mother."

When my friend indulged in one of his brilliant stanzas of deduction and logical thought, he still impressed me with the speed at which he was able to arrive at such ends. Chaplin, too, despite his anxiety, was wide-eyed in bewildered admiration.

"Sherlock Holmes, you amaze me! It is true; my poor dear mother, Hannah, has disappeared, vanished without trace. My friends, the Austins, tried to prevent her being taken from their house to the asylum, but when they went to that institution they found no trace of her. They wrote to me at the Mack Sennet studio but evidently their letter went astray. When I eventually got the news about a year later, I was unable to return due to the war. Then various events delayed this visit, but in the past few days I have made enquiries of everyone and everywhere seeming appropriate. It is obvious to me that all the authorities consider the passage of time too great. I made such a nuisance of myself at Scotland Yard that they put me in touch with a retired inspector of detectives of theirs, just to get rid of me I believe. He seemed, if you will forgive me, a little dull and elderly, but I will be eternally grateful to him for giving me your address and a letter of introduction."

The world's most famous actor needed no introduction, but handed one to Holmes. My friend removed the letter from its envelope and surveyed it for a minute or so. Then he handed it to me with a chuckle. I read:

My dear Mr. Holmes,

The bearer of this letter will, I feel sure, be recognised at once by one as astute as yourself; but just to be on the safe side, he is Mr. Charles Spencer Chaplin. You know, 'Good old Charlie', the same one that kept us all laughing even through that bloomin' blighter of a war!

He has tried to get them at the Yard to find his mother, who is evidently missing. They passed the buck on to me ... typical. Well, I can't help him other than with advice as my lumbago is something chronic.

Mr. Holmes, sir, I know you are retired well and truly, but I feel sure that you could make an exception for Charlie Chaplin who brightened our darkest days.

Look forward to meeting you and the Doctor again some day.
I remain, your humble servant,

George Lestrade

I could not disguise a smile as I handed the letter back to Holmes. My friend was hesitant in his reply. But seemingly after much thought, he spoke to the anxious actor.

"My dear Chaplin, Dr. Watson will tell you that I have made few exceptions in taking up any sort of investigations over the past seventeen years. In the main my only exceptions have been where patriotism was involved. But I feel that your work in cheering up the war-weary brings you and your affairs within that circle of exception."

I will be honest with my readers when I say that I was a little surprised by his words. Delighted, but surprised. As for Chaplin, that charming smile, that I would come to know so well, all but lit up the small sitting room. He could scarcely keep the excitement from his melodious voice – still very English save for the occasional American touch with the vowels.

"Mr. Holmes, I am delighted. I know that if anyone can find my poor dear mother, it is you. I confess that I had no idea when I arrived if you would help me, but in anticipation of a favourable outcome I came well prepared."

I had wondered at the bulge in the right-hand side of his jacket. I had doubted that he would carry a revolver, especially as he appeared to be right-handed. Perhaps Holmes already knew that it was caused by documents. He showered them onto the table – foolscap sheets, bulging envelopes and legalistic folded parchments bearing sealing wax and ribbon.

He explained, "On some of these sheets are the names and addresses of those who might be able to help. Also, there are details of local authorities and institutions. These are papers of restraint and confinement, and there are lists of places where she worked in a menial capacity, as well as theatres at which she appeared in happier times. All the addresses of homes we occupied are there, with details of dates. There is also a witnessed letter from me giving you permission to represent me in my absence concerning this matter."

Holmes nodded in approval. "So, you will not be present in England during the days to follow?"

"No, sir, I have to go to Europe, and thence to the United States, but having failed in the quest myself I doubt if I could be of much help. I leave it all with you, sir. There is an envelope in this stack, containing three first-class tickets for the *Olympic* sailing on the 29th of September for New York."

Holmes nodded sagely, "You mean that if I find your mother, I should use two of the tickets to accompany her to New York?"

"Certainly, and the third ticket is for a qualified doctor of whom my mother may need the services. Dare I suggest that Dr. Watson should fill this role?"

Holmes looked enquiringly at me. I said, "I have nothing to keep me in London, nor indeed in England for the immediate future. I would be happy to help. But, of course, I jump the gun a little; however Holmes may try, he may not be able to find Hannah Chaplin and the journey therefore pointless."

Chaplin shook his head. "I will want to discuss with you both at length concerning your attempts at least. Even if you do not find her, who knows what you might learn, and I will be anxious to confer with you both again. If you do bring my mother, it would be best for me to come to New York, where she could rest before making the long train journey to California. But if you are arriving without her, you can wire me to that effect and I will leave railway tickets so that you can join me in Hollywood."

My head was swimming; his words meant that regardless of Holmes's success or failure, I would be going with him to the United States.

Chaplin refused, with grace, an invitation to stay to lunch citing a prior engagement in London and we saw him to his Mercedes, an exercise which would hardly have occurred in the great days of Baker Street. I considered that country living had had a civilising effect upon Sherlock Holmes. When the big car was just a cloud of chalk dust in the distance, Holmes remarked, "A charming fellow, Watson, so hard to believe him to be a self-educated man."

I replied, "Generous, too, despite your reading of his footprint which led me to expect a skinflint."

As we returned to the sitting room, Holmes admonished me. "Where financial matters are concerned, I believe he is something of a Jekyll and Hyde. Did you notice how surly was his driver? Not a man who has been shown, or expects to be shown, much generosity. His early struggles have left their mark, save where his mother is concerned. His purchase of first-class tickets to New York is just a reflection of that feeling for her."

Holmes, ever the realist, was not to be diverted with dancing bread rolls, radiant smiles or tickets to New York.

We dined upon a steak pie with roasted potatoes, and green beans from Holmes's kitchen garden. It was excellent, yet I fancied I remembered Mrs. Hudson's steak pie as having a head start in any pie content. However, Mrs. McDonald's rolled currant pudding with hot treacle was perhaps the best I had sampled. I complimented the good woman upon her cooking and looked to Holmes for confirmation but he was preoccupied, saying instead, "I shall stay at the Charing Cross Hotel, Watson, and we can meet daily to confer. It will be good to breathe the tainted air of the metropolis again. Country life has made me rather too healthy."

After we had dined, we retired to the sitting room where Holmes sat on the bearskin, not from eccentricity but to give himself access to the Chaplin papers which he had spread upon the floor to form a rough circle. He sat amidst them, his great beak of a nose casting a shadow upon them, rather like an animated sundial. They soon became jumbled, yet I knew from experience that he could have restored their correct order within a few seconds.

I remarked, "Surely you can learn little from lists of names and places until you have visited or contacted them?"

He said, "I am not as yet investigating, Watson, otherwise you would already be complaining of the Scottish mixture. No, I am merely trying to immerse myself in the background of the Chaplin family." He lifted a document. "Here is a missive which commits poor Hannah Chaplin to a workhouse, and there are others referring to nursing homes and even asylums. Words on paper, Watson, but each one a tragedy in itself."

I dared to lift one of the scattered documents, but Holmes turned a gimlet eye upon me and said, "Watson, please!" I hastily returned the paper to its position in the scattered mass. He moved it a fraction of an inch to justify his admonishment and then said, testily, "Couldn't you go for a nice walk or something? Why not take a long stroll to Beachy Head, which I believe you have not yet visited. If you are brisk in both directions, you could be back in time for dinner."

I took a tweed cap from the hat stand in the hall, and beat a hasty retreat, pausing only to extract an ash cane from the elephant's foot by the front door. My friend had never made it clearer that he wished to be alone with his thoughts. At Baker Street I had learned to avoid such episodes through anticipation, but the passing years had made me a trifle out of practice in such diplomacy. When Sherlock Holmes describes me as his best, nay only friend, the reader will perhaps understand this better through the episode that I have just related. Were I of a more sensitive nature he might have had no friend at all: but truthfully I feel that one can make more than allowances when dealing with a man of Holmes's talent. On a different day, aye, or even a different hour of that same one, the episode would have taken a different path with my friend brimming with that charm that is also part of his character.

As it happened, I did react to his mood by mentally deciding not to take his advice for once. Instead of taking a southbound road I turned west in the direction of Ringmer. However, I soon abandoned the lane and took myself upon the Downs themselves, where the wind and the smell of the fresh grass soon dispelled any ill humour that I might have harboured. Despite my oft-mentioned bad leg, I was at the time still a considerable walker and found that by deciding my own pace I tired hardly at all. Eventually I took a southerly direction and made for Newhaven, a small coastal town which I have always enjoyed.

No enterprise there was grand enough for it to be designated a port, but there was a sort of harbour of great stones and steps down, where fishing boats lay at anchor and there were no pedlars of seaside buckets or purveyors of frozen confections. I sat upon the sea wall and took great breaths of air that was heavy with the aroma of ozone. Small boys angled for flounders from the wall with hand lines wound around square wood frames. One could soon spot the professionals among them by their use of much prized pebbles through which holes had been worn, enabling their twine to be threaded through. I remembered how sought after such pebbles were from my boyhood. They made splendid fishing weights, disguised as they were by their natural appearance. The barbless hook, fashioned from a bent pin cost nothing, and made the sport more splendid through the added difficulty of landing a fish with a hook that had no barb. As one of the urchins pulled up a flatfish that was more a plaice than a flounder, I was delighted to see that he had hooked this specimen with homemade tackle.

As I sat and mused upon the wall, I was tempted to hire a rod and line from the small double-fronted shop opposite. However, I resisted the temptation, feeling that in such company I might appear an old show-off. Instead I entered a public house, *The Jolly Fishermen* and enjoyed a pint of ale from a pewter tankard in a cool parlour. The landlord proved to be a large, seemingly happy fellow, but he took his humour a little too far. As I went to purchase my ale, my eye dropped upon a cardboard strip upon a shelf which bore the capital letters 'WYBMADIITY'.

"What does that mean?" I enquired.

He grinned, exhibiting a row of teeth like gravestones. He said (or seemingly asked), "Will you buy me a drink if I tell you?"

I said that I would and he said it was civil of me and poured himself a measure of spirit. I paid for my ale and his drink and then said, "You said you would tell me what it meant if I bought you a drink. Now perhaps you will tell me?"

He grinned. It was only then that I realised that 'WYBMADIITY' were the first letters of the words 'Will you buy me a drink if I tell you?' I smiled a glassy smile and said, "I see it now."

At which point the cheeky fellow said, "Then it's one up to you." So saying, he took a piece of chalk from his pocket and made a tick upon the lapel of my jacket.

This episode was made the more displeasing to me by the presence of a crowd of rough fellows who made sarcastic remarks concerning my ability to 'catch on'. I finished my ale and bade the landlord and his cohorts as polite a good day as I could manage under the circumstances.

I decided to return to Fowlhaven by a different route, keeping to the coast at least as far as Seaford. There I entered a cafe, which advertised itself as *Ye Olde Teashoppee* where I ordered a pot of tea for one and a teacake with strawberry jam. The elderly waitress, who was in fact the owner, explained that she had no jam, but some excellent honey. I found this unusual, but dared not stir up her evident perculiarities.

As I attempted to spread the thin honey upon my teacake, she asked, "Not from these parts are you, sir?" I said that indeed I was not. She said, "Thought so, the funny way you talk. Mind you, we do get quite a few visitors at this time of year. We call them 'comic-cuts'."

As I made my way back to Fowlhaven by way of the Downs, passing through a couple of picturesque hamlets, I mused upon how strange were the caterers of the south coast. The mild eccentricities of my friend Sherlock Holmes would seem quite mundane in comparison with what I had experienced in a single afternoon.

"Ah, Watson, good to have you back, my dear fellow."

I knew that his moods changed quickly, but proceeded with caution, enquiring, "I hope your research has proved helpful?"

Sherlock Holmes and the Charlie Chaplin Affair

He replied, "Helpful enough in that combined with Chaplin's narrative, the documents have given me a very good picture of his early life. There could be a detail, quite small, which will put me onto the right road in locating Hannah Chaplin. But I have put all of it away and we will forget the subject for one evening at least. Tell me, did you enjoy your walk to Newhaven?"

About to answer in the affirmative, I started, asking, "Really, Holmes, although I know your methods, I fail to see how you could know that I had walked to Newhaven when you had suggested that I make for Beachy Head."

He chuckled, "Well, Watson, I know you perhaps better than any man does, and remembering my boorish behaviour toward you I would guess that you would at that moment have taken anyone's advice save mine."

I was still puzzled, "There are many other places that I might have walked to."

"Indeed, Watson, but as it happened you walked to Newhaven, where you dallied at the harbour and then entered a public house known as *The Jolly Fishermen* where you had a joke played upon you by the landlord. You returned by way of Seaford where you paused to take afternoon tea in a café where the usual jam for the teacakes was unavailable. On the way back here you all but lost yourself, but by climbing a stile you found yourself on the right road. You took the Hailsham road by the way, and you made quite good time considering your adventures."

"Really, Holmes, you have had me observed in some way, because although I know the power of your methods, these details would be impossible to deduce."

He chuckled, "Not at all, Watson, when you leant over to charge your pipe from the tobacco jar, I could not fail to notice the grey cement-like dust upon your breeches. You sat upon the sea defence wall at Newhaven."

I gasped at his audacity which I felt now was making him disguise surmise as deduction. I said, "Is there no other wall in West Sussex upon which I might have sat to produce that effect?"

The Charlie Chaplin Mystery

He said, "Oh, certainly there is, but when combined with your visit to *The Jolly Fishermen*, it is clear where you had been sitting."

I rounded upon him, "But there is no way that you could know that I patronised that particular hostelry." (I waxed ironic.) "Or did I perhaps pick up some traces of beeswax from the polished stool that I sat upon. Come, Holmes, you are using guesswork, admit it."

He threw back his head and laughed, a rare occurrence with my friend. Then he gave me a full explanation.

"Watson, I have myself been victim to the childish prank played upon you by the landlord. Your lapel still bears a trace of the chalk mark which is its denouement. As for your return by way of Seaford, I admit that my knowledge of your ways was a great help. I know that you are partial to teacakes, spread thickly with butter and anointed with jam. I also know the good Mrs. Grace who owns and operates *Ye Olde Teashoppe* in Seaford. She is eccentric to the extent that she refuses to serve jam and dispenses only honey with her teacakes. She purchases her honey from me and insists that it is of a liquefied state, hence the stain left by a globule that must have landed upon your left cuff as you attempted to ladle the stuff. You then made for Fowlhaven by way of the Downs, losing your way and climbing the stile at Cope's farm, giving you access to the chalk road. I really must chastise Cope concerning those nail heads on his stile: I, too, snagged my nether garment at the back of the knee upon that access to the lane."

I said, "And my boots still show the signs of recent contact with the chalk. Really, Holmes, when you explain it, as ever, it is so logical and easy; but as the conjurer might say, 'It is simple when you know how'. Yet I never fail to be astounded by your extreme powers of observation."

Trying to play him at his own game, though only in the spirit of fun, I remarked, "I deduce that Mrs. McDonald has made us a splendid dinner of Irish stew."

A little later Mrs. McDonald served us with a delicious concoction of meat, vegetables and herbs, in a sea of succulent juices. When she collected the dishes, I complimented her, "A splendid Irish stew, Mrs. McDonald."

But she replied with mock severity, "I'll have you know, Doctor, that was a Hungarian goulash."

Holmes laughed loudly for the second time that evening, saying, "Upon my word, and I had thought that it was a Lancashire hotpot. You know, Watson, not only do all three of those dishes smell much the same when being cooked, but there is a great similarity in their taste."

Chapter Two

The Search For Hannah Chaplin

On the following morning another aspect of Holmes's frequent mood changes manifested itself. During the preceding twenty-four hours I had experienced Holmes the generous host, closely followed by Holmes the introvert, then a return to his cheerful generosity. Now I found Holmes sitting before me at the breakfast table.

"Watson, so good of you to put in an appearance. Pray deal with your scrambled eggs and coffee as quickly as you can, for we must catch the Victoria bound train from Brighton at eleven of the clock."

This then was the terse, 'game's afoot' Holmes of memory. The nostalgic pleasure he brought me was marred only by his extremely brusque manner. However, once we were in a taxi cab and on our way to Brighton station, he mellowed somewhat. He clutched a folder which contained not only all of the papers that Chaplin had left him but also his own notes and pieces of research. Once we were safely installed in a first-class smoking compartment at the station, he unbent to the extent of spreading the papers on the seat and did not show any objection to my own perusal of them.

He said, "Were I a writer, Watson, I would have enough here to write the opening chapters of a book on Chaplin's early life. Friends, employers, enemies, places of residence and institutions connected with the events of his life, they are all here in some detail. Fortunately, despite my retirement, I have kept up my scrapbooks from long habit. This quest upon which we embark together (and I fear I have as usual taken it quite for granted that you will join me), may well be a simple one, with Hannah Chaplin easily and quickly found. On the other hand, it could be part of a situation sinister or intriguing. Who knows? But I will have you know, Watson, that my return to such an investigation, be it long or short, wise or not, has quite brought the roses to my cheeks. I twitch at the nostrils, Watson, like an old warhorse that smells gunpowder after years of pulling a cab!"

It was quite an outburst from someone of Holmes's disposition and showed yet another side of the enigmatic erstwhile sage of Baker Street.

The journey passed quickly, its advertised sixty minutes seemingly passing like half that time; though I did manage to absorb quite a lot of the information that Holmes had gathered, once I realised that I was free to do so. Sensing his more amiable mood, I ventured to enquire, "What shall be our first move, Holmes?"

He said, "Well, first from Victoria, I will take a cab to the Charing Cross Hotel. You may wish to travel on to Finchley to check upon the serenity of your residence? Your stay with me at Fowlhaven was unfortunately short but no doubt we can remedy that when this Chaplin affair is concluded. I suggest we meet this evening for dinner at Simpson's in the Strand. I will pass the afternoon in meditating the task ahead."

I doubted that he would spend long in meditation once he had reached Charing Cross, but diplomacy prevented me from questioning this: if Holmes wished to spend a few hours left to his own devices in the metropolis, it was not for me to question.

Having telegraphed my housekeeper concerning my impending arrival, I was not received with any great display of surprise, save concerning the short duration of my absence. Mrs. Burrels was used to my ways save those where they concerned Sherlock Holmes. Where my late wife would have accepted the unexpected when Holmes was part of the equation, the housekeeper (an extremely domineering woman, whose competence is her saving grace) said, "I hope you did not fall out with your friend, Doctor."

I assured her that there had been no quarrel and that I would indeed be dining with my friend that very night. Evidently, she had cooked a pasty for my dinner but I managed to pacify her by taking it for a late lunch.

A few hours later I arrived at Simpson's to find Holmes already installed and faultlessly attired in evening dress tails, illustrating that a long sojourn in the Sussex countryside had not produced that rustic sloppiness so often accompanying such circumstance. He was for once hearty of appetite, saying to me, "What I pity you dined since I saw you, Watson, otherwise you would be able to deal with this pheasant pie as heartily as I!"

"Did I say that I had dined?"

"There was no need. You are a hearty trencherman and have merely picked at your savoury. However, we are not here to discuss your appetite. Since this morning I have not been idle. I took a ride on the top of an omnibus, partly because the experience is a rare one for me and partly to take in the atmosphere of mean streets in Lambeth and Brixton where Chaplin spent his youth. It has changed little in the areas in question from those times of the turn of the century. Children still run barefoot through filthy streets and dance around barrel organs begging for pennies. Elderly women trudge in carpet slippers, sporting their husbands's caps and holding a jug for the purchase of ale from taprooms. Men, unemployed save in the abuse of their wives and children, hang around street corners and desperate folk snatch what they can, pursued by irate tradesmen. Then there are those who are busily engaged in trade and commerce, costermongers, sweeps and purveyors of news sheets. There is noise everywhere and that rowdy bustle that is perhaps exclusive to that portion of our great city immediately south of the Thames.

"I tell you, Watson, although I have not seen it for years, it is all there still, just as if the Great War, which was to have been the great leveller of class and wealth, had never happened. The only sign of that conflict having occurred that I could see was in the use of the clothing with which people had been issued. The greatcoat of a 'Tommy' contrasting strangely with a coster's cap. The only sights of the past which I did not encounter were the strolling German bands and the Italians leading their dancing bears. The events of the past four years have robbed us or spared us of them, whichever view you prefer."

I asked him, "Did you at any time descend from the vehicle?"

"Why yes. I took to my feet on several occasions, Watson, wherever a district which figures in any way in our investigation presented itself, I walked the streets and all the time I observed. I must have climbed on and off more than half a dozen omnibuses. Today I began at the beginning, but tomorrow I will reverse the process, beginning at Hannah Chaplin's last known address: the house at Peckham. We will make an early start and interview the couple with whom her care was entrusted. There are aspects which Chaplin mentioned which have given me cause for deep thought. I would like to learn just exactly what her state of sanity, or lack of it, was at that time."

Later we strolled on the Strand and turned down to the Embankment. It was as if Holmes wished just to assure himself that it was still there. He lovingly inspected Cleopatra's Needle, that landmark which like London itself now bore the scars of some bomb shrapnel, but yet which did not really mar the general effect of this monument which had received worse treatment during the several thousand years of its existence.

As we climbed that steep little hill that is Villiers Street, we encountered a great many beggars and other unfortunates. The arches of the railway provident shelter for many such poor souls, especially noticeable among them the maimed and blind who were a dreadful reminder of the recent war which had caused their misfortunes. One could dispense a few coins here and there and be greeted with shaky salutes and mutterings to the effect that they were old soldiers. But we both realised that only some kind of government aid could go anywhere toward solving the problem. These desperate people hobbled, crawled or shuffled around, having answered their country's call, only to be told now that they were no longer needed. They had returned to the promised 'land fit for heroes' to find only lives as shattered as their limbs. Many of them had taken to drink and who could blame them? Of course, I imagine I had long known of these tragedies, but I believe it was only during that stroll with my friend that I came to fully appreciate the horror of the situation.

Then was we made for the entrance of his hotel, a final irony: a destitute man, begging for alms, who had managed to make himself look a little like Charlie Chaplin. He shuffled up and down swinging a cane and frequently raising his battered bowler and holding it insinuatingly for the collection of coins. I was forced to laugh as I slipped a coin into his hat. But Holmes was not amused, saying, "Watson, a professional humourist dressed as a tramp is amusing, but the real thing is tragic. When Chaplin appears thus attired, one suspects that in fact he and his garments are actually clean."

It had all become a little deep for a simple soul such as myself, so I took a nightcap with Holmes and then returned to Finchley in a taxi after having promised to join him on the morrow.

As it happens that day dawned exceedingly damp and miserable, but I knew that my friend would not rejoice in any excuse I might make to defer our meeting. Inclemency of weather would scarcely deter him in his plans. Indeed, when he greeted me, he was already clad in a waterproof garment of the kind said to have been invented by a Mr. Macintosh, and hat which matched it in style and purpose. He glanced at his pocket watch just as severely as he glanced at me as he returned it to its pocket.

"Really, Watson, punctuality is, you know, the politeness of kings. However, I am sure there is good reason for your delayed arrival so we will mention it no more. Now let us seek a taxi cab and be on our way."

"You do not intend to again take the omnibus?"

"No, Watson, time is not on our side, although I am still glad of the experience of yesterday. Pray, button the neck of your coat, Watson, for I see that the rain is now descending quite heavily."

He was right and I was glad when the third vacant cab appeared as we repaired to the Strand. (We evidently still had to follow the golden rule concerning cabs, even now that they were motorised.) Holmes gave the driver the address in Peckham where we were to seek Chaplin's friends, the Austins.

Thanks to the wonders of modern engineering science, we had reached our goal within a quarter of an hour. To my dismay, Holmes paid off the cabby evidently with no thought for our welfare in the event of the Austins not being available. But he read my thoughts as he so often did.

"Watson, surely you did not think I would neglect to telegraph concerning our visit?"

The house was a big Victorian one, several floors with a slate roof, detached from those around it and standing in its own grounds. The front garden was composed mainly of an untidy shrubbery. There were steps up to the front door, tiled with a black and white chessboard effect, and the front door itself was of a once light oak finish but darkened with age. I noted that the door and steps had seen attention, yet the front garden had not been tended for months. I tried to picture Mrs. Austin, a sedate house-proud woman with her husband not at all inclined to rake or hoe. I doubted that they had domestics to do these things. However, I was wrong upon all counts, for the door was opened to us by a typical skivvy in a mob cap and holding a duster. When I say 'typical', I must say that with reservation. She was somewhat middle-aged for a domestic and very slow on the uptake. Holmes handed her his card and said, "We are expected by Mr. and Mrs. Austin."

The woman dabbed at her face with the duster and then vanished, presumably to inform her employers of our arrival. This had the effect of producing an elfin-like woman of perhaps five and forty with heavily hennaed hair and a tweed jacket and skirt of unfashionable length. She welcomed us pleasantly enough.

"Mr. Holmes, Dr. Watson, pray do come in. I am Ada Austin and you will meet my husband in a minute or two. Please come into the parlour. Make yourselves at home. I will get the foolish girl to make us some tea."

We sat where we were bade in a bright parlour at the back of the house. It was a pleasant enough room, made the more so by framed theatrical memorabilia upon the walls. Most of the posters seemed to include 'The Austins ... Ada and George', but there were several which bore the name, among others, of Lily Harley which I had learned was the professional *nom de théâtre* of Hannah Chaplin. Framed photographic portraits also adorned the walls, mostly depicting The Austins, Ada almost unrecognisable in her motley. George appeared as an athletic young man. They appeared in the portraits to be performing some kind of comedic acrobatic act, but then George Austin entered and introduced himself, explaining it all.

"Gentlemen, I see you are intrigued by our portrait gallery. Ada and I did our comedy acrobatic routine in music halls in the winter and circuses during the summer. That way we always had work, for the better part of twenty years."

There was an interlude whilst the 'foolish girl' who evidently rejoiced in the name of Gladys brought us tea on a tray. She needed supervision I noticed even to perform the act of depositing the tray upon the table. Ada explained, when the retainer had left, "Gladys has been with us for many years. She is a bit slow, but a willing soul. She got left behind by a couple who stayed with us many years back."

George took up the theme. "You see, when we retired from the show business, we had been very careful and had saved our money, which meant we were able to buy this house. It was very run down and we have put a lot of work into restoring it. However, it took all that we had been able to save so we opened it as a boarding house, and have operated it as such ever since. As Ada says, Gladys got left behind by a couple called The Gilpins who had a riding act. Gladys was her sister, I believe, though it's hard to be certain. They stayed here often enough, but the last time they scarpered the letty."

I did not understand the meaning of this phrase, but Holmes nodded. "Theatrical slang for decamping without paying the rent, Watson. So, Mr Austin, you were unable to trace these Gilpins; surely they must have continued in traceable theatrical employment?"

"I fear not, Mr. Holmes. I heard on the grapevine that they had gone to Australia and changed the name of their act. Of course, the sum they owed us was not terribly important, but we just did not know what to do with poor old Gladys. We never have quite decided, so you see her still with us as a sort of companion housemaid. If she had to leave us, she would end up in an institution. The poor girl doesn't deserve that."

The Austins struck me as being very kindly people, and the subject of Hannah Chaplin crept quite naturally into the conversation when Holmes pointed to a professional portrait of a young woman in a theatrical gown, attractive and seemingly lively from the pose. Although the name Lily Harley was imprinted below the portrait, it was inscribed in ink 'To dear Ada and George, love from Hannah'.

George explained, "That was poor Hannah in her soubrette costume. Good little artiste she was, and you will see that she could do character songs too; if she had been able to control her nerves, she could have been a second Lilly Morris or Marie Lloyd perhaps. See from the other pictures; all in character."

We glanced at a composite of portraits showing Lily Harley in turns as a sporting lady complete with badminton racquet, an old woman with a cloth apron, a male impersonation as a dandy, and a flirtatious girl, looking over the top of her fan. Holmes studied these carefully before asking, "You speak of her nerves being not quite strong enough to endure the life of a touring artiste for very long. Was it through stage fright or did the troubles manifest themselves in other ways?"

It was Ada who said, "Mr. Holmes, you did not know her husband, Charles Chaplin Senior, as one now needs to call him since Charlie became a big star. He was a spendthrift, a drunkard and a dreamer who led the poor woman a terrible dance with his debts and escapades. Charles was very talented, could earn good money not only as an artiste but as a song writer. But he spent his money faster than he could earn it. He and Hannah and the two boys were forever having to move house to avoid paying the rent. In fact, it became quite a legend in the business, didn't it, George?"

Austin continued the narrative. "Ada is right. Artistes would hand their music sheets to the band conductor on the Monday morning and say, 'There you are, it's Chaplin's third movement from not paying the rent'. He was notorious in the profession for such things."

I ventured, "Why do you think Hannah stayed with him so long?"

"Because she loved him; he was a very charismatic man. He never treated Hannah or the boys badly, and he accepted Sydney, who was Hannah's son by a previous marriage, as his own. In fact, she never would have left him. It was he who left her in the end. Having the two boys to support and her natural nervous disposition got the better of her in the end."

Ada took over again. "It started, the troubles, when bailiffs called and she was forced to fob them off with stories of expected monies from influential relatives. In the end I don't think she knew truth from her own fiction. Do have a scone, Doctor."

As I accepted a scone, George took over the story.

"Through the years the boys were taken from her because she had retreated into a world of her own. They had to go to a local authority boys' home, not always together. Yet miraculously the three of them always seemed to be reunited. Several times Hannah had to go into hospitals and even asylums, but the boys always seemed to get her back. Once they had gone into the show business themselves, they had helped her enormously and when Syd and Charlie were both with the Fred Karno troupe, she was even able to tour with them. Her nerves got a lot better, but when the boys went to America she had a relapse. Syd came back, got her out of a nursing home and brought her to us. We looked after her and then they sent us money regularly. They were both able to get back to see her until the war started."

It was Ada's turn to continue the narrative; they were clearly a double act.

"They were trapped over there because for much of the war America was a neutral country and as such could not allow belligerents to return home. Not that Charlie or Syd were belligerent, two nicer boys you could not wish for. Then, doubtless because of the blockade by the German submarines, we didn't even get letters from them. As soon as the war was over, Syd came and paid us the money they owed, but Charlie was too busy to be able to get away. Not that it would have made much difference because she was taken to the asylum quite suddenly, just before the end of the war."

Holmes had not interrupted their words until this point, doubtless in case he should gain some scrap of information as yet unknown to him. But now he started to ask questions.

"She was taken I understand by ambulance men who had documents to support their action?"

"That's right, but Ada will bear me out that they were a motley-looking crew."

"George is right, they were all different shapes and sizes. One of them was practically a midget and another could pass as a giant. Then there was a very stout one and only one of them was what you might call average."

Holmes started at that and enquired, "There were four ambulance men to take away one frail elderly lady?"

"We thought it a bit strange. Mind you, Hannah was far from frail by that time; we fed her well."

Ada showed us a sepia photograph of a rather plump-faced woman who looked to be in her fifties, with short white hair and a rather bemused expression. It was difficult to tell that this indeed was a picture of Hannah Chaplin when comparing it with the Lily Harley portraits. Holmes delved into the leather satchel which he carried. He brought forth a document with a local authority heading.

"Was the document anything like this?"

They perused it, but were both a little bit vague on the subject. "Something like it, I suppose."

"Not exactly the same."

I thought to enquire, "Did Hannah Chaplin come and go as she pleased or did you discourage her from going out alone?"

George and Ada agreed, "Our arrangement with the boys was that she was never to leave the house on her own. We were gently firm with her over this because Sydney had told us that the authorities would take her off to a home if she got in the slightest trouble. Even though she had become so much calmer, we had to stick to the rules. But one or other of us took her for a walk each day, wherever she wished to go."

Holmes was rather thoughtful as he said, "Strange then that she had managed to get herself in some sort of trouble for the authorities to claim her after so long?"

It was a statement rather than a question. They agreed that it was so. Holmes asked, "How did Hannah herself react? I mean did they carry her away kicking and screaming or did she go with them quietly?"

"Oh, she went quietly enough, but she did appeal to us to stop them taking her, didn't she, George?"

"As you say, Ada, she went quietly, and the fact that there were four men made it easier for them to carry her belongings and put them in the ambulance."

This reply made Holmes thoughtful. He said, "That is unusual, for in such cases the relatives or guardians are usually asked to send belongings as required. Tell me, did you keep her room for her after she left?"

George was very definite upon this point, almost as if it was an accusation rather than a question. Ada appeared to bristle a little too as George made his reply. "Of course, we kept it for her. Indeed, as the boys have paid for it, even including for the years she has been away, we keep it for her still."

Holmes's eyes widened. "May we see it?"

"Certainly. Ada will take you up there."

As we climbed the stairs to the top of the house, I enquired, "Did you try to visit Mrs. Chaplin at the asylum?"

I thought that Ada Austin seemed a little guarded in her reply as she said, "Well, we tried to but we were told that we would have to leave it for several weeks before we could see her. But since the boys went there and were told she was not a patient, we have not been there again. Ah, here is Hannah's room. Of course, she took a lot of her clothes with her but they were mostly the things in her old property box, quite unsuitable for everyday use. If you look in the wardrobe you will see that they did not take most of what I would call sensible clothes."

Holmes looked in the wardrobe and agreed that the clothes therein were of the kind that one would have expected her to need. But I was more interested in seeing her collection of photographs which were pinned still to the wall. There were a number of them, the expected pictures of herself with her sons in the early days, one of Charles Senior ('To my darling Hannah') and some which were clearly of artistes, perhaps a past circle of friends. A strong man lifting a barbell, a woman with performing dogs, a midget performing acrobatics, a plump Italian tenor and others of the kind. All were signed to 'Dearest Hannah' in various handwritings. Hannah had also evidently left various bits and pieces of her personal property – an alarm clock, a pen set and inkwell, a writing pad and a small box of cheap jewellery. My friend examined them all with interest, even holding the top sheet of the writing pad up to the light. He said then, "My dear Mrs. Austin, you are to be congratulated upon the spotless nature of this room. Obviously, you clean it still each day?"

"Why, yes, I like to think that poor dear Hannah could come back at any time and feel at home again. Do you think you can find her, Mr. Holmes?"

My friend was more than gentle as he replied to her obvious care and concern.

"Rest assured, dear lady, that I will do everything in my power to discover what has happened to Hannah Chaplin. Remember, I have quite a good record in that direction."

As we bade farewell to the Austins I had the feeling that whilst they were obviously concerned for Hannah Chaplin, they could also have been slightly relieved that they no longer had the responsibility of her welfare. After all, the care of one mentally abnormal woman must have been headache enough for them. I mentioned as much to Holmes who seemed undecided upon the point.

"You could be right, Watson, though I fancy that the money which evidently Chaplin still pays them to keep the room for her must be useful. I saw no sign of frenzied activity concerning other lodgers or paying guests. But for the moment we must give them the benefit of any doubt."

We repaired to an eating house, evidently much frequented by cab drivers judging by the number of taxis outside as well as the odd surviving horse-drawn hire vehicle – no hansoms but one or two four-wheeled cabs. As we entered there was an atmosphere caused by a great many pipe smokers that you could have cut with a knife. It was reminiscent of the sitting room at 221B Baker Street in those halcyon days of the three- and four-pipe problems. Holmes revelled in it and taking out his pipe and tobacco was shortly contributing to the fog of smoke as we drank scalding hot tea from large mugs. The food and drink was dispensed by a large florid-faced man in shirtsleeves and an apron who blew periodically through the jungle of a moustache which decorated his upper lip. He had a genial manner yet tempered it with a certain sternness.

"Righto, Captain, what can I get for you and your mate?"

Holmes whispered to me, "An ex-sergeant of the Royal Engineers. He recognises you as an ex-army officer, but cannot place my position in society. He was demobilised with a pension and was therefore able to open this pull-up for car men."

I ordered two plates of fried gammon with sausages, fried bread, beans and fried eggs. His manner mellowed, especially when I tried out Holmes's deductions, or rather their validity.

"I am glad to find you busy, Sergeant. A bit of a change from laying cables and pipes on the western front."

He all but saluted as he made his reply. "Mostly they have come in for a smoke and a fourpenny one if you get my meaning, Major? (He had decided to promote me.) If it was not for my pension I doubt if I would get by. Still 'san fairy ann' as we always used to say, eh?"

I soon had made inroads into this splendid plateful and as I started to consume it, I asked Holmes, "Clearly a sergeant, but how did you identify his regiment?"

"From the regimental badge design of the tattoo on his right forearm. Not difficult to spot, Watson. He limps, indicating a wound which would bring a pension. He 'copped a Blighty one' as his army colleagues would have called it; moreover, it is clear, as he himself has stated, that this place would barely give him a livelihood were it not for his pension. Will you be taking anything to follow your snack?"

I had noted that Holmes had left quite a lot of his meal upon his plate but I was not going to let him shame me into failing to partake of the plum duff which I saw advertised upon a chalk board. I said as much and Holmes chuckled as he made to order the pudding for me. When he returned with a steaming plate of suet pudding and custard, ('just what the doctor ordered' as the sergeant would doubtless have described it), he said,

"Watson, Hannah Chaplin has been here in this very eating house upon a number of occasions, though not during the last four or five years. Evidently, she used to come here with Gladys when that unfortunate lady was given charge of her. According to the sergeant this was the only café in the area where she was welcome due to her tendency to break into vocal impersonations and renditions of music hall songs. He says that she specialised in emulating Lily Harley, an artiste well known during his youth. As Hannah used that name professionally there can be little doubt that he speaks of her.

He also assures me of something that is significant, Watson: he seems convinced that Hannah was in charge of Gladys."

At once I could see why this suggestion interested him, but he explained anyway.

"To the casual observer, aside from her vocal eccentricities, Hannah would appear quite normal when moving in society. Perhaps she made recovery beyond that ever dreamed of by her sons?"

I could see his point: in order to find Hannah Chaplin, we would need to cease centring our search upon the supposition that we were seeking a lunatic, or even an eccentric in the extreme sense: yet oddly our next move was clearly to visit the asylum to which the Austins believed her to have been taken.

Institutions designed to house the insane are always extremely grim, especially those operated by the authorities to which disturbed persons are taken, usually against their will, through the issue of a court order. Such a place was Cane's Hill Asylum, situated on an incline and presenting even from its exterior a depressing edifice. We were received politely enough, but the official who dealt with us struck me as being somewhat guarded. Due to my medical qualifications, Holmes insisted that I should be the spokesman, and I explained to a Dr. Marsh just who we were seeking.

"We are trying to trace Hannah Chaplin, a lady who was a patient here but whom we understand is no longer with you."

Marsh fidgeted with discomfort as he replied, "I believe I explained to her sons that to my knowledge she was not here at all in recent years. I let them see my files, which showed her being admitted and discharged from this institution a number of times before the outbreak of the war. There was some disruption in our system during the period of that terrible conflict with most of our staff being called to military service or to work upon other essential labours connected with the war effort. To be bluntly honest, there are no files at all to cover the period which interests you. But I have been working here for the past six to seven years, and I can assure you that Hannah Chaplin was not admitted during my sojourn."

"Could she, though, have been admitted under another name, perhaps as Lily Harley?"

"I think not. The lady was described to me by her sons; in fact, they showed me photographic likenesses of her in late middle age and I would have recognised and remembered her. I suggest you consult the legal people at the Town Hall. I'm sure they must have kept their files in order even in wartime. Please forgive me, but I am busy and must leave you now."

As we left that bleak place, Holmes remarked, "A man with a guilty manner, and yet I doubt that he is in fact guilty of anything save incompetence. We will follow his suggestion, which was indeed already upon my list of priorities. But first, I want to talk to the ambulance men."

It was Holmes who this time took up the questioning as we halted by the ambulance, which stood in the drive of the asylum. There were two of them, both rather dour, middle-aged fellows wearing rather dingy white jackets. One sat upon the step of the driving cabin as he smoked a hand-rolled cigarette. The other was standing uneasily about as if expecting to be observed, and tinkered with a stretcher which leaned against the side of the vehicle. They both shook their heads when Hannah's name was mentioned but brightened when given each a half crown by my friend. However, there seemed little that they could tell us, but when Holmes described the ambulance men whom we believed had brought her to Cane Hill, they were more forthcoming.

"There is only the two of us, also Fred and Alfred who work when we are off. Never more than two of us, and one of us the driver at that. Fred and Alfred are both average when it comes to height, build and appearance and as you can see, neither of us is extra short or unusually tall. No lofties or tiches work here."

Holmes considered, "Is there any chance that the vehicle itself might have been, shall we say, borrowed for a few hours at a time?"

"Not over the past ten years, guv'nor; Bill and I lock it safely in the old coach house when we have done with it. Fred and Alf do the same."

As we descended Cane's Hill, I asked, "Do you believe them?"

"I have no reason not to, Watson, for all is pointing now toward that which I had already expected. In visiting the Town Hall, I simply follow the expected pattern. I do not believe that any sort of order concerning Hannah Chaplin has been issued in the past seven or eight years."

"But would Chaplin and his brother not have known of this?"

"Evidently not, Watson, which shows us how trusting of authority they both still are, even after a nightmare childhood in which asylums, orphanages and workhouses figured."

At the Town Hall serving Camberwell we learned that Holmes was correct in his supposition. He could learn only of a great many long past orders of restraint against the lady we were seeking. These corresponded with the copies of documents that we had.

We took a cab back to Charing Cross where we dined in Holmes's hotel. After a rather splendid meal (roasted mutton from the bone, sauté potatoes and baked cabbage with vinegar sauce followed by a melon glace with ginger and gruyère cheese with biscuits), we sat in the magnificent lounge and took coffee and liqueurs. Of course, we discussed and contemplated all that we had learned during our day of investigation.

"Holmes, you really believe then that there was no official warrant or order for the restraint of Hannah Chaplin?"

"My dear Watson, surely you must yourself have come to that conclusion."

"Do you mean that you believe that she was abducted by person or persons unknown as yet; and if so, what possible motive could there be? Ransom? After all, Chaplin is now a man of great wealth."

My friend shook his head. Lovingly he stripped the band from a Havana cigar and cut one end of it with his penknife.

"Do you imagine that any person or group of people might abduct her for that purpose without putting any of their cards on the table by now?"

"Maybe they abducted her and failed to treat her well so that she died? In which case we are seeking murderers ..."

"Such morbid thoughts had occurred to me as well, Watson, but without any real evidence to back up such fears we must assume that she lives yet; concealed in a manner and for a purpose that we have not yet discovered."

"So, despite much activity we have learned next to nothing?"

"Hardly so, Watson." Holmes lovingly blew a blue plume of cigar smoke and then replied.

"My dear fellow, we have learned a good deal which may or may not assist us in our quest for Chaplin's mother. Let us begin at the guest house of the couple known as the Austins. They were a seemingly forthright couple, yet one got the feeling that they were holding back about something. We had been led to believe that Hannah was mentally deranged, yet the owner of the café frequented by her and the poor girl companion would seem to have a slightly different story. The asylum to which she is supposed to have been taken have no record or memory of such an event, and their own ambulance men were clearly not those described by the Austins, either by their number or appearance. So, who and what do we seek, and which way do we turn now? You appear to believe that we have come up against a stone wall, yet I believe that the wall has gaps in it if we can fine them. If you wish to sleep upon such thoughts do not let me detain you. As for myself, I shall continue to ruminate, aided by nicotine and small occasional measures of spirit."

I took his hint; the hour was late and I was ready for bed anyway.

Chapter Three

A Distant Light

When I neared the Charing Cross Hotel upon the morning which followed, I was intrigued to see Sherlock Holmes, standing before the newspaper and magazine stand upon the pavement outside the building. He gave me one of his typical crablike sideways greetings.

"I could not find what I wanted to see on the bookstall within the hotel, but this vendor has more catholic tastes. I trust you slept well, Watson?"

Having dealt with all such niceties as he appeared to think necessary, he picked up a copy of a periodical titled *The Era*. He dropped some coins into the vendor's outstretched hand and led me to the entrance to the railway station. There he made for the refreshment rooms where he bought me some coffee and took a hot chocolate for himself. "My preferences have changed a little, Watson, in recent years; age seems to make me seek sweetness – possibly the proximity to honey has something to do with it?"

I said little, knowing that he might well change back to his more usual paths by teatime. However, I was curious about his purchase of a copy of a periodical usually read by vaudeville and music hall artistes. I asked about this and he said, "Watson, Hannah Chaplin, or Lily Harley, was in her younger days a variety performer of some note. I just wanted to see if *The Era* might inspire me to think as she might. If not, it will make a change from the *Thunderer*?"

I tried to occupy myself by glancing at the back cover of the paper as he held it before his face. But I could learn little from it as it appeared to be composed of professional name cards of variety performers – 'Carlton, the human hairpin', 'Happy Fanny Fields' and 'George Robey, the prime minister of mirth'. The latter name was well known to me but most of them were not. Then, when Holmes put the paper down flat upon the marble table, he pointed with his pipe stem at a column of 'Variety Agents cards'. He indicated one name.

"Charles Foster, agent to the stars", his address is in the Strand, Watson, not a stone's throw from where we sit."

"Thinking of going on the boards, Holmes? Maybe you would do well with a thought-reading act, or with a troupe of performing street arabs: 'Sherlock Holmes and the Irregulars'?"

The remark was meant in jocular fashion but my friend was in a rather more serious frame of mind than I had realised.

"Upon my word, Watson, can you not realise that if we were seeking a missing designer of houses *The Architects Journal* would perhaps be helpful? Because the variety performers are there to entertain and beguile us does not mean that they are not real people deserving to be taken seriously when trouble befalls them. Come, this Charles Foster may well be of great assistance to us."

Much chastened, I followed him along the Strand until we came to a building near the corner where Fleet Street begins. We ascended what seemed like endless flights of stairs until we reached the door upon which was emblazoned the name Charles Foster. We entered the waiting room of the man whom we would soon understand to be a leading light among theatrical agents.

"You a double act?"

A girl at a desk made the enquiry in a voice which told me of her acute sinus condition. She sniffed into one of a pile of cambric squares which lay before her on the desk.

I replied, "No, we are not a double act ..."

"All right then, what do you do?"

"I'm a doctor ..."

"Doctor of music, magic or mesmerism?"

Holmes was tired of this repartee and said, "Good morning. I am Sherlock Holmes ..."

But as it happened, he had only made the misunderstanding worse, as illustrated by her reply.

"Oh, I get it, Sherlock Holmes and Dr Watson? Well, you are both a bit long in the tooth but the get-ups are good and I suppose you could get away with saying that you were them as old men. (She yelled through a half open glass door ...) Mr. Foster! There is an act out here that is unusual. At the very least might be good for the number twos."

Charles Foster emerged, a tall heavily built man, immaculate of attire with the carefully dressed hair and manner of a showman. He gave us a half smile.

"All right, boys, what do you do?"

It was the girl, however, who answered. "They do a routine as Sherlock Holmes and Dr Watson."

He was interested now and asked, "Is the patter any good, and is there a good song to round it off?"

I opened my mouth to protest, but Holmes intervened.

"Watson, let me deal with this, there is a misunderstanding."

I replied to the effect that he was more than welcome to deal with the impresario, but our converse became mistaken for stage dialogue. If only Holmes had not decided to wear his Inverness cape and deerstalker against a cold autumn wind.

Foster said, "All right, you look right and you sound right, and I have the right by-line for the act. How about 'Elementary, my dear fellow'?"

When Holmes corrected the misunderstanding by the presenting of his card, he all but made the matter worse, as Foster said, "The real thing? You hear that, Helen, they really are Holmes and Watson. Even better."

I could see that my friend was fast losing patience with a situation, which at first had promised to be merely amusing momentarily. Now he was becoming less calm, though obviously I realised that he was astute enough to know that he could hardly lose his temper completely with someone from whom he desired to extract information (though just what it was that he required of a theatrical agent was still beyond my ken). But Holmes was ever the diplomat, especially when he was aware that it suited his purpose.

"Mr. Foster, my friend and I did not come here to seek theatrical employment, nor are we desiring to book any music hall turns. All we ask is a little information to aid an investigation."

Foster looked disappointed, but yet could see the funny side of the situation. He laughed, and said, "I realise now that I jumped the gun a little, but of course the girl led me to think you were an act. Now that I stop and think about it, I realise that it would be a little undignified for you to be a turn. After all, with all those exploits written about you in *The Strand*, you are both institutions, and I don't mean like Pentonville and Bedlam! Good name for an act, Helen, make a note. Come into the office, gentlemen, I will of course help you in any way I can."

He led us through the glass door and seated us in two extremely uncomfortable chairs. As he sat down himself and faced us across the table, I realised that his own extremely comfortable-looking seat was raised up on a small platform. He had the advantage of looking down at us as we fidgeted on our hard seats. He noticed our discomfort and apologised.

"Sorry about the chairs, gentlemen, but with most of the people I deal with it does not do to make them too comfortable lest they are here for the day. I learned that from a book on business methods. The author also suggested that the businessman should be seated higher than those he interviews; intimidating I think was the word he used. Now, Mr. Holmes, what can I do for you?"

Holmes brought forth a photograph of Hannah Chaplin as she had been at the height of her theatrical abilities. He passed it to Foster who recognised Hannah at once. I remember wondering if Holmes was doing the right thing in coming so close to putting his cards on the table. I noticed, however, that the picture bore no name, either genuine or *nom de théâtre*. Foster studied it and brightened at once.

"Why, it's Lily Harley! Nice little soubrette, good voice when the wind was in the right direction. I booked her quite a bit, she was never a star but quite popular and could have done better if she could have handled her nerves. Aside from that she had a couple of kids that she took everywhere with her, and that didn't help her either. I got the impression that her husband had run off and left her with them. Mind you, I would have continued to book her despite that problem, but the nervous trouble affected her voice too much and too often. Not much more I can tell you about Lily except that I have not clapped eyes on her in nearly twenty years."

It became clear to me now that Holmes had wanted first to establish if Foster knew that Hannah was the mother of the now world-famous Charlie Chaplin. It was obvious that he did not and Holmes gave him no sort of prompting in that direction. Indeed, when he handed him the picture of Hannah in middle age, there was still no name to provide a clue.

He said, "This is a portrait of the same lady as she appeared just a few years back. She is missing and her family have asked me to try and find her. I have reason to believe that she might attempt to return to the theatre in some capacity or other."

Foster studied this second portrait with great interest and compared it to the first that he had been handed. Then he said, "Poor old Lily. Mind, I can see that it is her despite the fuller face and the white hair cut short. Well, Mr. Holmes, if she had any thoughts in that direction, I imagine I might be the first agent that she would think of. But what would she do? She certainly would not, I imagine, try to resume where she left off. I suppose she might try character work, get a small part in a play as a duchess or a charwoman. Elderly actresses usually specialise in those sort of parts."

Holmes said, "Should she contact you with something of that kind in mind, I wonder if you would contact me at the Charing Cross Hotel? If she does come to you, please do not alert her to my quest, but try and make another appointment with her so that I might be present."

Foster looked thoughtful. "She has done nothing wrong, I mean you are not going to have her arrested?"

"Nothing of the kind."

"Good, then I am happy to cooperate. You know in this business we don't sneak upon each other to the authorities."

"The news I have for her is good, but I must give it to her in person. Confidentiality is essential."

I wondered if this matter had been Holmes's sole reason for his visit to Charles Foster's agency. But he answered my thought with a further enquiry.

"Do you by chance have any posters or programmes of the appearances for you made by Lily Harley?"

After a certain amount of delving into cupboards and alcoves, Foster produced about a dozen showbills, headed South London Palace, Argyle, Birkenhead, Folly Theatre, Manchester, Collin's Music Hall, and so on. Each of these bills proved to bear the name of Lily Harley, though not at its top. There were other names, but most of these were not repeated save for one act titled The Jolly Bakers, which appeared upon several of the posters. Holmes quickly noticed this as if it was that which he was seeking.

"Mr Foster, did you book this act, The Jolly Bakers?"

"I did indeed, a good turn, there were four of them, dressed in white and covered with flour. Lots of slapstick with the pastry dough and so on. I used to book them into pantomimes too. Brokers men or comic policemen and so on."

Holmes was clearly interested in The Jolly Bakers, enquiring, "Could you describe them, their physical appearance?"

"I can do better than that."

Foster opened a desk drawer which all but overflowed with photographs. He spent two or three minutes searching among them until he came forth with a photograph measuring about ten inches by eight or nine, depicting four comical figures in white coats and pale faces. It was obvious that one of the four was unusually tall and another of them was extremely short. He placed it before Holmes on the table with a gesture of triumph.

My friend studied it with great interest and then pushed it in my direction, saying to Foster, "I take it they are pale from the application of zinc oxide?"

Foster's eyes opened wide at this display of knowledge. He said, "Correct, you obviously know something about theatrical make-up. Funny you should mention it, but the boys were all extremely pale of complexion offstage too. There is something about zinc oxide which makes it very difficult to wash off. For example, most circus clowns are extremely pale. Just as you can spot a coal miner, you can always spot a clown. Like soot, you never quite get rid of it all."

I remembered with rising interest the way the ambulance men had been described to us. It was hard to believe that Holmes had held some thought about this that was now confirmed. As we shook hands with Charles Foster, and left he called after us, "Just think, if I booked you at a theatre, I wouldn't even need to tell you which one or where it was."

At this point Holmes led the way to *The Cheshire Cheese*, a long-established hostelry in Fleet Street. It had an all but basement tap room made cool through its flag-stoned floor. There was the smell of aged timber which blended with the fumes of ale.

Holmes explained, "This was the coffee-house where Dr. Johnson used to confer with Boswell. I thought it might be nice for Sherlock Holmes and *his* Boswell to visit here."

Holmes has a pixie-like sense of fun which he exhibits rarely, but I feel the reader will appreciate this particular example. However, I was anxious to talk with him about what he had learned from Charles Foster.

"The description of the four ambulance men had a theatrical ring, Watson. I cannot, however, insult your intelligence by saying that I deduced this from the fact that they were pale of face. It was the contrast of heights being so extreme that put such an idea into my head. I believe that upon the morrow we need to visit the Austins again."

"You believe then now that Hannah Chaplin was abducted?"

"We discussed such a possibility before, Watson, but now I am beginning to think that we are dealing with an escape rather than an abduction. I believe that Hannah wished to leave the care of the Austins for reasons as yet unclear."

"Maybe she felt the restriction of so many years of that which can only be called a house-arrest?"

"Possibly, but she may have wanted to leave without raising too many questions. Had she simply walked out of the house without returning a hue and cry would have resulted. But the Austins, she may have felt, would not put up any great resistance to her removal by the local authorities to the asylum. It is possible that she staged the whole thing to gain time before any great search might begin. If that is so she has indeed gained her wish. She may also have not wished to bring public attention to herself as the mother of the famous Charlie Chaplin, for his benefit rather than hers. They were close indeed when he was younger."

"You mean she did not wish to see a broad sheet headline to the effect that Chaplin not only has a lunatic mother, but that she is missing?"

"Exactly, Watson, and this raises the point that Hannah Chaplin, if she thought upon these lines and took the steps which I suspect can hardly be described as a lunatic."

"You mean that she is now mentally improved through long rest and freedom from worry?"

"We cannot be sure, Watson, but have you ever considered that there might have been very little wrong with her mind from the start?"

I caused our tankards to be recharged and then answered his question.

"You have in your satchel perhaps a dozen court orders to restrain her as a person mentally deranged."

Holmes charged his pipe with the Scottish mixture, and as he tamped it down in anticipation of the application of a lit match, he said,

"You are a trusting soul, Watson, as far as the establishment in general and the local authorities are concerned. Understand, I do not suggest corruption, although it may exist in isolated pockets. Rather I suggest actions brought about through convenience. Cast your mind back many years and imagine yourself a town clerk, mayor or chief constable. You are constantly being presented with the problem of a sick woman, suffering perhaps nothing more serious than that which would today be referred to as a nervous breakdown. She has two young boys and her husband, who is a drunkard, is permanently absent and refuses to contribute to the welfare of his family. He is a popular affable man despite his intemperance. She is delicate and bursts into floods of tears whenever, as frequently happens, her sons are taken from her on a temporary basis. Eventually they ill lose patience and have her confined for a short period to a mental hospital. They expect that when she is released either she, or her children, might have become somebody else's problem. Eventually they realise that they must periodically repeat the process if it is to have any effect. Later still, they certify her as a lunatic and have her confined to an asylum. These institutions are full of poor souls, Watson, some of whom may need to be there for the safety of themselves and others, but there are many who are there solely because they are an embarrassment, to either their families or the authorities. I believe that Hannah Chaplin may come within this category."

It had been a long and considered opinion, made by an outwardly cold and ascetic man. But such people can secretly have very kind hearts – such a man is Sherlock Holmes.

We passed the remainder of the day looking at the displays of advertising photographs exhibited outside the central London theatres and music halls. I realised that Holmes was searching for the likeness of any actress bearing the slightest resemblance to the lady we were seeking. After an hour or so I protested, "Holmes, I am sure you have taken into account that in the doubtful event that Hannah Chaplin has tried to resume a theatrical career, she could as easily be appearing in the provinces. There are I believe several thousand theatres in Great Britain; we can only catch sight of cast photographs at a very few of them in this way."

Holmes was peering at a group photograph of the cast of *Floradora*. He looked up and coldly remarked, "Chance has often played a good part in my career, Watson. I follow my instincts, my dear fellow. I follow my instincts. But there is nothing to stop you from returning to Finchley. Come, we can meet up again tomorrow."

The reader may be horrified to learn that I took Holmes up upon this offer. I can only plead that my leg was giving me pain and that I was beginning to realise that I was not as young as I had been. So, making my apologies and the appointment for our meeting, I hailed a cab with the intention of going directly to my home in Finchley.

It so happened that the cab took me by way of Clerkenwell and Farringdon, doubtless heading for the Holloway Road. Then as we skirted Islington Green, I spotted on my left the little music hall known as Collins (doubtless named after the original owners). Holmes and I had visited the theatre, said to be the oldest established variety house in London, many years before when investigating a matter for the famous comedian George Robey.

On a whim I decided to descend from the cab and dismiss it, knowing that I could very easily get another. I wanted to inspect the publicity photographs outside the theatre. I could see no portrait that one could conceivably have taken as a depiction of Hannah Chaplin at any stage in her career. Thinking that I had seen all the pictures, I made to turn away when I noticed that I had missed one or two freestanding frames which were leant against the base of the entrance. These were frames belonging to the artistes themselves and conveyed from theatre to theatre as they toured. The first featured Nellie Wallace who appeared as an extremely quaint-looking woman dressed in a tricolour jersey and short tweed skirt below which could be detected a pair of knickerbockers. She wore a Robin Hood hat from which blew a long feather; with hands clasped in supplication, her prominent nose up thrust, she looked very strange indeed, though according to the posters she was the top of the bill and her name was traced in electric bulbs across the facade. Another frame had four pictures of a comedian, Bert Elmore in various characters from a cleric to a dustman.

But then I saw a third frame which really did present me with some interest. It contained a group photograph of four men in white coats and pale faces. They were holding large pastry rolls. One of the four was exceptionally tall, another very short indeed and the other two could have passed as being of average height as far as could be seen. My heart leapt, feeling that in searching for Hannah we had forgotten to look for The Four Bakers. However, the act, according to the title on the frame and the bill matter on the posters was The Doughboys: yet I realised that the name of an artiste or an act might be changed to suit topical tastes. During the conflict mercifully passed the American servicemen in Britain had been referred to by many as doughboys, and the four eccentrics might well have realised how good a title this would be for an act centred upon a bakery. I could not wait until the following day to tell Holmes of my discovery, so I took a cab back to the Charing Cross Hotel as quick as I could.

I instructed the driver to follow the Strand from Fleet Street, hoping to discover Holmes, still inspecting theatre lobbies but instead I spotted him outside the hotel itself.

"My dear Watson, have you forgotten something? I would have by now expected you to be seated comfortably in your study or taking an early dinner. Or perhaps you suffered with your conscience in leaving all the footwork to me?"

But he soon dropped his irony when I gave him my news.

"The Four Bakers are playing at Collins's Music Hall, not two miles from where we stand, but they are now called The Doughboys."

He clapped me on the shoulder in genuine admiration. "Oh, well done, Watson, how did you make the discovery?"

"By chance ... I stopped the cab at Islington Green to look at the photographs ..."

"Hardly chance, my dear fellow, you were tired out, yet still alert enough to have our quest in your mind. The Four Bakers had slipped my mind in being so single-minded in the search for Hannah." He looked at his pocket watch. "Come, we can be there for the second house, if you are up to it? I seem to remember that you enjoy a vaudeville performance from time to time."

"I used to as a student but haven't been inside a music hall since that Robey affair."

"Well, now is your chance, Watson, to relive a few happy memories."

"I am scarcely dressed for the theatre."

"Nor I, but I imagine we will not stand out among Collins's patrons. As I remember, the atmosphere is free and easy."

So saying, he hailed a cab and surprised the driver when he gave him the destination. That worthy asked, "Are you sure Guv'nor?" He shrugged when Holmes repeated our goal.

Collins's historic music hall appears to have been built onto the side of a public house bearing the same name. Indeed, despite the facia one enters through an alley between the two buildings. The prices are modest, as is the fare offered, but it is of the kind which appeals to, and satisfies, the locals who reside about Islington Green. Holmes was right in his assertion that our daywear would pass muster for I spotted not a single person in the theatre sporting evening dress. The young men wore serge suits and collarless shirts with white neckscarves. Their hair was plastered to their heads and some sported buttonholes. As they sat in rows beside their 'Dona's' with their flowered hats, they exuded an air of anticipation of enjoyment to come. The older men wore flat caps, which appeared to be part of their heads, and the older women sported leg of mutton sleeves and Dolly Vardon hats of a previous age. They were, I suppose a typical second house audience, distinct from the slightly more downtrodden and smaller first house group that we had watched shuffling out as we bought our tickets. 'Two front stalls, luv? Rightcha!'

I recognised the lady in the ticket office from her mittens and two pairs of spectacles.

Although the six-piece orchestra in the pit played an overture selection of music hall melodies, the show itself was variety, or what our transatlantic cousins would call vaudeville. Indeed, the American influence was there, with several of the artistes assuming transatlantic accents. There was a French act which went very well; Madame Fifi's Pets which proved to be half a dozen rather dejected-looking poodles. I found it rather depressing as the dogs rather unwillingly jumped small gates and burst through paper hoops; but the boys from the pit shouted '*Oo la la*' as Madame Fifi wriggled her hips. Nellie Wallace was an old favourite, a superb comedienne, or perhaps 'droll' would be a better word to describe her. She sang to the effect that the following Monday would be her wedding day 'To little Percy Peckitoff who lives across the way'. The repeat chorus was her opportunity to break into a mad dance in which she displayed the famous sacking knickerbockers. Then she went into a monologue touched by innuendo, which was heightened by quick little movements of her hands. A consummate artiste I thought, but I could see that Holmes was anxious to see The Doughboys.

First, however, there would be an interval during which more old-time chorus songs were played during the dropping and raising of the metal safety curtain. Some magic lantern slides were projected onto a small cinematograph screen: 'George's Pie and Eel Shop ... just one minute from the theatre' and 'Pearson's High Class Fruiterers ... by appointment to the public'. We did not repair to the bar due to the obvious fact that patrons were all but swamping this facility.

Although we had a programme with numbered items, this was not strictly in the order of the artiste's appearance. One had to wait for a lighted number to appear at the side of the stage to know what one would see next. Gone was the chairman of music hall, variety was a more quick fire medium, the second half commencing with The Dancing

Daughters, three girls dressed as sailors and dancing in unison. There were other turns, but eventually the Four Jolly Bakers, or 'Doughboys' as they were now known, came bouncing onto the bijoux stage.

Sherlock Holmes sat forward in his seat as the four comical performers threw themselves and each other around. Fast music accompanied their antics and the curtain before which they had entered parted to reveal a trestle table bearing huge wads of pastry dough, a rolling pin, a wooden spoon and a huge saucepan. The four of them began to knead pieces of the pastry and throw it around, mostly at each other. The tallest of them, who must have been a little in excess of six and a half feet, balanced his smallest partner in a variety of ways, then jumping onto the trestle he laid upon it, raising his legs into the air with the little fellow supported by his enormous feet. He juggled the little man upon them much as I have seen done with barrels by other performers. I cannot recall all that they did, but I can remember that after a slapstick interlude in which they all became covered in dough and flour, they formed a kind of pyramid wherein the big man lifted the other three, one with each arm and the little man standing upon his shoulders. It was the kind of turn that in a West End theatre could have fallen flat, but here at Collins's on Islington Green, it was greatly appreciated. As they took several curtain calls, I wondered what Holmes would decide to do next. I had not long to wait to find out.

"Come, Watson, the stage door."

I followed him, and we left the auditorium whilst Nellie Wallace was making her second entrance, dressed this time as Anne Boleyn, singing of hilarious goings-on at the Tower of London.

"Do you intend calling back stage to question these fellows?"

"For the present, no, Watson, for we know where to find them. For the moment I prefer to observe their departure, its manner and direction."

We stood across the street at a point where we could observe anyone leaving the theatre by the stage door. We

A Distant Light

were using a parked vehicle which made convenient cover. Then within a minute Holmes's gimlet eyes had taken in something which I had overlooked entirely. Upon the door of the driving cab there was sign written The Doughboys. The rest of the vehicle was painted white and at a glance could well have been mistaken for an ambulance. Holmes took his lens to the sign writing and declared, "The words were obliterated with whitewash at one stage, Watson, which has since either worn or been washed away. I believe we are looking at the very vehicle which conveyed Hannah Chaplin away from the home of the Austins. The fact that their stage costumes could be mistaken for those of hospital workers may have put the whole plan into their minds."

"But why did they do it? No ransom has been demanded of anyone."

"There are aspects of the whole thing which are curious, Watson, but for the moment our problem is to find where this vehicle will be driven when its owners drive it away."

Sherlock Holmes is usually beyond reproach when it comes to observing the letter of the law. Yet there have been times when he has taken extraordinary and illegal steps when the game has been afoot. This was one such occasion. The back of the van was secured with a padlock and having assured himself that he was unobserved, Holmes opened this with his penknife. (Not difficult when dealing with a simple padlock as any owner of one who has mislaid its key will agree.) He swiftly opened the double doors and peered around the inside of the vehicle. It was all but empty save for a few typical stage properties and, not surprisingly, a sack of flour. I was somewhat on edge, expecting the four acrobats to appear beside their vehicle at any moment. But Holmes worked quickly, moving the flour sack so that it was immediately central and near the double door. He made a swift movement with his penknife, piercing the flour sack so that a small amount of the white powder spilled through. He arranged it so that the hole corresponded with a small gap in the base floor, near the spot where the centre of the doors would be when they were closed. I had no idea what he was doing but he illustrated this by closing and relocking the doors and pointing out a small trickle of flour upon the road below.

"You see, Watson, if my plan succeeds, we can let them have a start so that they will not suspect they are followed. But then we can do just that almost at leisure. My first idea in opening the back of the van was to conceal myself inside so that I would learn where they were going and make a diplomatic retreat after they had left the van. But the sight of the flour put another and, I believe, better, certainly less dangerous thought into my head. When the vehicle is driven away it will, with luck, leave a trail of flour."

"Upon my word! Perhaps you could sell the idea to Chaplin to use in one of his photo plays?"

Holmes chuckled, but then became serious again, saying to me,

"Quick, Watson, they are returning to this vehicle. Retreat, my dear fellow, in the direction of the cab rank."

I did as he bade me to and had only the chance of a momentary glance at the returning quartet of comedic acrobats. All I could notice was that they were in street clothes, but still looked extremely pale. Once we were thirty or forty yards away, we risked a casual observation. I had been concerned that they might open the padlock and Holmes's scheme be thwarted. But only two of them were evidently travelling in the van and they entered its cabin. They were the very tall and very short man, the two who were of average height waved casually and walked in the direction of the green. The big man inserted the handle below the front of the bonnet of the van and gave it a turn whilst the little fellow adjusted the arrangements at the driving wheel. After a shudder or two the engine started and the big man climbed into the cabin. The van was soon on its way and to our joy it left a thin trickle of flour upon the road.

"We will engage a cab to follow the trail, Watson, and for once in my life I will take the first on the rank, because I recognise the driver."

The cab driver raised his eyebrows a little when Holmes asked him if he could follow the thin trail of flour. He was none too happy about this until my friend revealed his identity. Then the reaction was electric.

"Why, Mr. Holmes, I haven't seen you in twenty years or more. Fancy you remembering old Fred Hawkins. I was still driving a hansom in those days, and I often wish I still was. Whoa, it's the doctor, too ... jump in, gents, we had better get going."

The driver was obviously intelligent enough not to follow too close to the back of the van. In consequence it sometimes turned and disappeared from view but the trail enabled us to always catch it up again. While this was happening, Hawkins beguiled us with stories of his life since we had last had contact with him.

"Remember the old horse, Ginger? Well, early in 1916 some blighter from some government department or other presents himself and says that he is commandeering him for military service. I ask you, taking a poor old cab horse to send to the western front? Well, I was too old for the army really, but I had no livelihood without the horse and not the price of another even if I could have found one. So I told them at the recruiting office that I was ten years younger and that my birth certificate had been eaten by mice. They didn't believe me but they took me on because they were so short of men. I spent two years on the western front but never ran into Ginger, though I kept a good look out for him. Hello, your quarry is slowing down, Mr. Holmes, I'd better not get too close."

The small man had jumped down from the cabin of the van (no mean feat for a man with such short limbs) and was entering a house in a terrace. Holmes noted the address in his notebook, and as the van started off again we continued our discreet shadowing of it.

"It's going to head south ..." Hawkins was alert and we continued behind it at a respectful distance as the driver's narrative recommenced.

"When I got demobilised, they found me a job driving this thing. Fortunately, I had learned to drive an army lorry, and if you can drive one of those through mud and over blown up roads, you can drive anything. Then I got a wound in my leg, thought with luck it might be a Blighty one, but it soon cleared up thanks to an excellent nurse – Enid, she ended up as my old woman."

The flour trail was declining as the van drove relentlessly south. Hawkins opined, "He's making for Brixton, if not beyond." But Brixton it was and the van stopped at a run-down Queen Anne-style house with a crumbling portico.

At the time of which I write the south London district of Brixton held probably the largest collection of theatrical lodging houses in the capital and this followed a long-established tradition. These varied from well-kept houses to those which were all but falling apart from neglect, with financial charges equally varied. The house near which we had stopped obviously came into the latter category. We waited half an hour to see if the tallest Doughboy should emerge again but it eventually seemed clear that he was almost certainly lodging at the disintegrating villa. That it was a lodging house we established when we saw the printed 'Vacancies' card in one of the front lower windows.

We journeyed northwards again, dropping Holmes at Charing Cross. After arranging to meet him on the following day, I continued on to Finchley.

Chapter Four

'Pro Digs' in Brixton

I was awakened by the insistent and irritating ring of the telephone. I never have cared a great deal for this modern mode of communication. However, as a medical man I could not refuse to be connected to the system for long. As I was no longer in regular practice, I hardly had occasion to use the instrument, which gathered dust in the hall of my home. It was eight o'clock and I knew that I alone would need to rise from my bed and answer – both domestics being truly alarmed still at the idea of conversing with a disembodied voice. I lifted the earpiece from its cradle.

"Hello, John Watson here …"

"My dear Watson, an amusing spectacle you make as you stand there pulling your dressing gown around you."

It was indeed Sherlock Holmes, his voice sounding even more incisive than when he was speaking at one's shoulder.

"Holmes! The telephone transmits the voice, but any sort of picture is yet to be invented. How can you tell that I am in my dressing gown; does it rustle?"

"Possibly, though I have not discerned it. You have hurried to the telephone, for you answered it quickly and you were gasping for breath as you did so. Therefore, I deduce that you were upstairs, probably in bed. I know you well enough to assume that you would not display yourself before your servants in your pyjamas. You really must train them to answer it for you. No matter, I am calling to remind you of our appointment at the *Bear and Staff* at one o'clock. Might I ask that you bring a Gladstone with a change of clothes and your soap and razor? Just enough for two or three days."

"You mean, the game is afoot?"

"Well, it is for you at least, my dear fellow. But I will elucidate when we meet."

There was the click, which meant that Holmes had hung up the instrument at his end. There was no way that Holmes was to be argued with upon the telephone, any more than when he was there in person.

After breakfast I informed my housekeeper that I might be away from home for a couple of nights and that during my absence she must conquer her fear of answering the telephone. Then I dressed in a town suit, packing a jacket and breeches, shirts and toiletries in a Gladstone. I was determined that I would remain quite cool when I met with Holmes, and make no enquiry as to our destination.

For once time was on my side, and I made my way to the West End upon the top deck of an omnibus. I had, of course, travelled by this means quite a number of times, far more often than had Holmes. But I admit that I had been far more often upon the horse buses, which had disappeared soon after the turn of the century. In those times if seats there were vacant, one could sit next to the driver and talk with him as he held the ribbons and whipped the boys who tried to hang onto the side of the vehicle. Now the driver was on the lower deck and isolated from his passengers who were not supposed to distract him in any way whatever. One could, however, still chat with the conductor if he was not too busy, as he circulated with his wooden ticket trough. It was on the whole an extremely pleasant experience to ride on the top of a bus when the weather was not inclement. To feel the breeze in one's face was refreshing, but when the rain was falling and the seats were consequently damp, one only rode the top deck if the bus was unusually crowded.

I climbed down at the top end of the Charing Cross Road and walked the last mile down that fascinating thoroughfare with its bookshops on ground level and theatrical agents who operated from the offices above. Famous actors and well-known music hall performers rubbed shoulders with the ordinary business people and sightseers in one of my favourite London streets.

Then just before Trafalgar Square and on the Leicester Square side of the road I came upon the *Bear and Staff*, a cosy public house where one could sit in an alcove in private conversation. In such a booth sat Sherlock Holmes, who beckoned to me as I entered the hostelry.

"My dear Watson, you are very punctual. Pray, be seated and I will myself fetch you a tankard of the best brew." He was very amiable and I began to feel that he was breaking gently toward informing me of something bad.

"Well, Holmes, perhaps you can tell me now what your exact plans for me might be? Your telephone message was both terse and intriguing."

Holmes sipped from his tankard and blew through his pipe prior to charging it.

"Have you ever held any sort of secret desire to be an actor, Watson? I have often thought you would make a splendid character man."

"Holmes, surely we need to get down to the matter in hand rather than dwell upon whimsicalities?"

"Oh, I do not speak in whimsy, Watson. I need to put someone I can trust into a certain Brixton lodging house; someone who can report to me about several matters from within. I would pose as an actor myself, but I feel my face is rather too well known, and as it would doubtless be for a very short period I feel sure that you would be up for the challenge."

At once I grasped his purpose. If a fellow thespian were to get upon friendly terms with the tall member of the Doughboys's troupe, various things might be learned, perhaps just dropped in conversation if Hannah Chaplin were mentioned without pressure. I assured him of my compliance and added,

"Will they not expect me to be engaged in some theatrical endeavour?"

"Not necessarily, Watson, the profession is largely made up of unfortunates who are almost permanently 'resting'. They never seem to give up hope. The part that you must play is that of such an optimistic character actor. Each day you must leave the house and pretend to be looking for suitable employment. If you ask the other residents for assistance it will make you the more convincing."

"Do you not think that I should get a special wardrobe that will make me appear to be down on my luck?"

"Not at all, an actor's clothes are the tools of his trade, rather like the plumber's wrenches, kept spick and span to the last." He was, oh, so persuasive.

I will spare the reader the rest of the arrangements that were made and the arguments indulged in. To cut a fairly long story short, it was agreed that I should take myself to the crumbling guest house that we had seen the night before. Holmes would accompany me in a cab which would stop a street or so away. If within fifteen minutes I did not reappear, Holmes would assume that I had managed to rent a room and that I would present myself at the Charing Cross Hotel at noon the following day.

As we travelled to Brixton by cab, Holmes explained that his own plans included investigating the activities of the small Doughboy, whose place of residence we had learned the previous night.

As I walked up the gravelled drive of Vaudeville House – the blades of grass almost outnumbering the pieces of stone themselves – it was, I confess, with some trepidation that I knocked upon the door. It was opened by a small, but old lady who asked,

"Hello, dearie. Looking for digs?"

This made my task far easier as I had only to agree. Holmes, with his many strange contacts had a friend in St Martin's Lane who had a small hand operated printing press. He had leaned upon him to produce a dozen or so cards with 'Barrington Carstairs – Character actor' embossed upon them. ("An actor without cards, now that would be unbelievable, Watson!") I presented one of them, which after peering at it short-sightedly she handed back to me saying, "You want to hang on to them, dearie."

Right there on the doorstep she told me that it was five shillings deposit and two shillings a night. She further explained, "You'll get a good breakfast and a snack when you gets back from the theatre."

She held her hand out palm upward and tickled it with the forefinger of her other hand in a most insinuating manner. It was obvious to me that she expected the deposit at least before I would be allowed even to enter the house, let alone inspect the room. I decided to place two half-crowns upon her palm, making a show of searching my pockets. After all, Barrington Carstairs would not be exactly overburdened with wealth.

She led me up a carpetless staircase until we reached a landing with several doors. She opened one of them and indicated for me to enter a fairly large room in which five beds were easily enough accommodated without it appearing to be a dormitory. As I dropped my Gladstone onto the bed which she pointed out, I realised why she had wanted the deposit before showing me the room. My knowledge of theatrical lodgings was practically non-existent, and in my innocence I had expected a room of my own, but I said nothing.

"You'll be all right here, dearie ... I don't have no roughs or drunks or anything like that."

I did my best to seem reassured as I made some sort of play of unpacking. There were no wardrobes, but I noticed that the other presently absent occupants had used great ingenuity in hanging garments from picture rails and judicious use of string and drawing pins. An outsize suit of clothes hung over one of the furthest beds from my own told me, without much recourse to the science of deduction, that the largest Doughboy lodged in the room.

Leaving my partly unpacked bag upon the bed, I ventured forth upon a voyage of discovery. There were two other rooms, no doubt similarly housing a number of beds and a smaller door marked 'Bathroom'. A carpeted stairway to the top of the building suggested to me that the owner of the establishment possibly dwelt up there. Downstairs I found a dining room at the front and a sitting room at the rear. The front room was extremely basic, housing a long trestle table and a dozen or so chairs around it, but the sitting room, although shabby, exhibited a certain degree of homely comfort. There were several sofas and easy chairs that had seen better days, a few footstools and a low table bearing aged copies of *The Era*, and other professional papers and magazines. A musty smell throughout the building appeared to me to be caused by damp, which seemed to have attacked much of the wallpaper. I decided to seat myself and allow the situation to develop on its own, rather than to pursue any particular course of action.

I suppose I must have nodded off in the least mouldy of the armchairs when I was aware of being addressed by someone. It was a female voice which startled me out of my half slumber.

"Hullo, dear, haven't seen you before. Just arrived, have you?"

I arose and inclined my head as she seated herself upon one of the sofas. She was a woman in her mid to late fifties with short grey hair and a rather waif-like face. She was dressed in a sensible tweed skirt and a woollen cardigan. She was matter of fact rather than over-friendly for which fact I was relieved. I answered politely, "Why yes, I am Barrington Carstairs, and I arrived just about half an hour ago. Just been inspecting the accommodation, what?"

"Not up to much is it, but I've known worse digs, love. Mind, I can only speak for the girls' room but I imagine the boys are in a similar rather primitive situation."

"It is a little Spartan, but it seems to be clean enough."

"Are you working or resting, love?"

"Resting. I'm looking for a part for an elderly thespian such as myself. Are you working yourself?"

She shook her head dolefully and said, "No, but I have every expectation of something turning up. I have a son in the moving picture business and I hope to be going to California to join him eventually. But that may not be for some months yet and I, of course, would like to work if only to pass the time, let alone so that I may go to Hollywood with some money in my purse."

My heart started to beat; had it been so easy for me to find Hannah Chaplin? If it was so I could not believe my good fortune, but controlled my excitement so that it could not be detected. I enquired of her, in as casual a manner as I could manage,

"Dear lady, might I enquire your name?"

"I am known as Ada Foster professionally, but my real name is Ada Harding. My son is Robert Harding. He plays a lot of small parts at the Sennet studio, but he knows Chaplin quite well and as Charlie has broken away from Sennet to make his own pictures, there is every chance that he will get better parts in Chaplin pictures. As soon as that happens, he is going to send me the money for my boat ticket."

I wondered, were she in fact Hannah Chaplin and trying to remain incognito, would she be likely to even mention the Chaplin name? I thought it unlikely but could not rule out the possibility that I had found the woman we were seeking. I was careful to keep the conversation upon a general track.

"I suppose you don't know of anything suitable for an old gentleman that might be going?"

She shook her head but said, "I'll look out for something when I see my agent tomorrow."

"You are most kind and I will of course keep my eyes open in case I hear of a part for a gentlewoman such as yourself."

Her eyes opened wide and she adopted an arch manner, "Why, thank you kind sir, she said. Wait until old Charlie Foster hears how you have described me."

"You know Charles Foster?"

"He is my agent, duffer."

"Of course, I should have realised."

"Do you know Charlie? Don't tell me he is your agent, too?"

"Oh, no! But I know his reputation, of course. You must be a very accomplished actress to be represented by him. Have you been with him for long?"

"Oh, not that long, a year or two, but you see I was out of the business for a number of years. I was originally a music hall artiste – used to call myself Maggie Masters. But you know how it is, love, my act relied upon youth and beauty, and those are things that don't last forever. I had a nervous breakdown, which kept me out of business anyway for a year or two, but then when I recovered, I decided to become a character actress. I have done quite well, and no one has seemed to recognise me as Maggie Masters. Well, here I am telling you my life story and I don't know anything about you, Barry."

I started. It had not occurred to me that people would shorten the name Barrington to Barry, but I made light of it.

"Oh, there is not much to tell you, Ada, you see I came into the business fairly recently. (How true that was!) When I retired from my job at the Ministry of Agriculture, I decided that as I had always wanted to be an actor, here was my chance."

She chuckled as she replied, "Ministry of Agriculture ... manure and all that ..."

"We call it fertiliser ..."

"There and I thought I was being polite calling it manure!"

Obviously, the lady had a Rabelaisian sense of humour, but she soon stemmed her chuckles and said, "You know, I would have taken you for a military man."

I was startled. How much more of my background was obvious?

"Well, in my youth I served in India and Afghanistan."

Rather to my relief a third person joined us, and by coincidence he proved to be the huge man from the Doughboys. Close up I was fascinated to see how the flour and its constant use had given him the pallor that made him appear unhealthy despite his robust build. He nodded to me, and Ada Foster made the introduction.

'Pro Digs' in Brixton

"Carl, how are you doing? Oh, by the way, this is Barry. He's an actor. Resting he is, and we both know what that is like."

The big man seemed good natured and easy to get along with.

"Good to know you, Barry. I am one of the Doughboys, and we are at Collins's this week. Next week, however, we are also resting, but after that we have a week at the Argyle Theatre at Birkenhead and after that we are at the Bedford, Camden Town. Then we rest, perhaps until the pantomime at Huddersfield, ja?"

He was Germanic, but with very little accent. I tried to learn what I could without seeming to pry.

"So, you are at Collins's this week? A lovely little theatre, full of character and history."

"Backstage it is full of history; there are some very large old rats which infest the dressing rooms. But you, Barry, are legitimate, no?"

Ada laughed immoderately again and made the obvious innuendo.

"If Barry and I are legitimate, what does that make you?"

Carl laughed and said that it was a very funny joke, but I could tell that he was laughing to be polite.

"Upon my word, is that the time. I must take the van and meet the boys. Then we will just have time for a snack and must make for the theatre. They have switched us to opening turn for the first house." He had glanced at one of these modern wrist watches and I consulted my hunter to confirm that it was four o'clock. After he had left, I chanced my arm by asking Ada a few questions about the Doughboys.

"Have you known Carl for long?"

"Bless you, yes, I used to run into them all the time in my music hall days. They were the Baker Boys then, but changed the name after the war. Poor old Carl was interned, you know, during the whole of 1915 and 1916 due to one of his parents having been German. Then after a couple of years they realised how harmless he was and he was even doing shows at troop concerts in the end. He did a single for a while, but then after the war he reformed the act, though with different partners. It is his act, you know, he pays his partners every week even when they are resting. Otherwise they would be off working somewhere on their own. We all have to make a living, don't we?"

"That must be very difficult for him financially, to pay them when they are not working."

"Well, that's why he gets them doing odd jobs when it's slow. They have that van, you see, and with it the four of them can use it for all sorts of purposes. They move people's furniture, and I've even known them drape it with black material and use it as a hearse. Once they even used it as an ambulance, I believe, though I don't know the full story."

Again, I tried to be casual, even when hearing such things, which were of great interest to me.

"I have seen their act, (I did not say where) and the little man works well with him."

"Oh, Little Jimmy, rather! He is essential to the act, whereas almost any competent acrobats can stand in for the other two."

"Yet this Jimmy does not stay here?"

"No, Jimmy likes to be away from the others. Most dwarfs are temperamental, you know."

"I would have called him a very small man rather than a dwarf: I believe four foot five is the line of distinction."

"You sound more like a doctor than an actor, Barry."

I realised that I had been unwise in the way I had used my words. Fortunately, however, she was just being jocular. However, I felt that I needed to cut short my conversation with Ada Foster before I really did put my foot in it. I made some excuses, saying that I had to meet a friend who might manage to help me to secure employment. Remembering my character, I made as jaunty an exit from the room as I could. Then I made for the nearest park where I sat upon a bench and considered all that I had learned. This was quite a great deal and I could hardly wait to unburden myself to Holmes the next day. It was possible that I had actually discovered Hannah Chaplin, and if I had, there seemed no danger of her

'Pro Digs' in Brixton

decamping in the immediate future. Even if I was mistaken about this, I had at the very least confirmed the suspicions that we had held concerning the Doughboys and their bogus ambulance.

Knowing that my first opportunity of meeting the entire lodging population of Vaudeville House would be at the after-theatre snack time (which I estimated as perhaps between eleven o'clock and midnight), I resolved to find some useful way to occupy myself until that hour. Finding a café, I decided that having some sort of a meal was as good a way of passing an hour or so as I could think of. The place I found was hardly Simpson's, but provided an excellent dish of sausages, mashed potato and beans. I was amazed at how much of it there was in a single portion and how nimble was the price.

Eventually I solved my problem concerning the killing of time in a way which I felt would combine business with pleasure. I came upon a picture-theatre, where some of Chaplin's films were being shown. Although I had, of course, met Chaplin, I had never seen him upon the silver screen: indeed, my visits to such places of amusement had been few indeed and scarcely ever had I visited a proper Kinema. I had seen films shown in booths at fairgrounds and at Maskelyne's, but that had been in the infancy of the invention. The theatre was titled The Picture Dome and seemed to be quite professional in its style. I paid a shilling and entered the cinema. My shilling seat proved to be at the back of the auditorium, the sixpenny ones being where the stalls would have been in a theatre. The performance proved to be continuous.

My seat was comfortable enough, but I found it disturbing that whenever words appeared at the foot of the screen to accompany the action of the film, these were read aloud by many persons in the sixpenny seats. It seemed as if the near literate were reading the words for the benefit of illiterate friends. They needed to shout the words that they might be heard over the noise made by a more than lively pianist who appeared to have a somewhat limited repertoire – *Devil's Gallop* for a chase and *Daisy Belle* for romantic scenes.

As for the films, they all featured Charlie Chaplin but appeared to vary considerably in their quality of production. There were films that shook and shivered upon the screen and those that gave the impression that everything took place in pouring rain. As there were also some films that did not trouble the eyes and did not shake, I assumed that I was seeing a selection of Chaplin's work which spanned a number of years. He had told us that he now produced and directed his own moving pictures so I decided that the erratic films were some that he had made for others. The subject matter varied, sometimes the scene was a skating rink, or a bakery, or a park, on a promenade or in a ballroom. The supporting actors were extremely energetic and far from subtle. The same flapper-type girl appeared again and again as did a small cross-eyed man, and a huge fellow who seemed always to be the villain. There was also a moustached policeman who appeared again and again, and a shorter upholder of the law who contrasted with him by making balletic movements. There were dangerous dogs, which fixed their teeth firmly into the seats of actors' trousers, and horses, which looked as if they were fit only for a knacker's yard.

But through it all shone Chaplin himself who I had to admit was really quite superb. Not just obviously funny, but deeply so in a manner which could make one cry as well as laugh. He seemed to me to portray a harmless little fellow who tried to deal with everything that fate flung at him to the best of his ability, uncomplaining to the point when he could take no more. Then he would rebel and strike back, but still in a manner which seemed extremely fair. He was the defender of the weak against the bullies, yet always in an amusing way, and he rescued damsels in distress heedless of their ingratitude. Much put upon, he would still smile and tip his hat prior to waddling away in his own hilarious way. The twirl of his cane and the shrug of his shoulders would ever be the final view of him as he walked off into the sunset. This little tramp was so unlike the Charlie Chaplin that we had met at Fowlhaven, save for that off-screen charm of his which now and then crept into his work upon the screen. Now I understood why Chaplin had in a few short years become not only a big star of the silver screen but possibly the best-known single human being in the world.

Although I made no conscious attempt to remember the names of the supporting players, their names appeared so often at commencement of the films that I could scarcely fail to notice their repetition: Eric Campbell, Norma Talmadge, Ben Turpin, Mildred Harris, Edna Purviance, Mack Swain, Hilary Lyle and others. I will confess to the reader that as the performance was continuous, I was not just able to see some of it for a second time, but I actually did. Reluctantly I left the theatre, slowly backing out, past the booth from which the film was being projected. I was conscious of the sound made by the projector as the film clicked through its mechanism, being merged with the pianist's music and the cries of laughter and amazement from the patrons. I took one last glimpse of Charlie as he flirted with the girl on the park bench and managed to accidentally poke the huge policeman who stood behind him with his cane. As I stepped into the street, momentarily dazzled by the daylight, I realised that I would probably be a devotee of the cinema for ever more. As I walked, I noticed more than one small boy performing a Chaplin-style walk, one of them with even a borrowed cane and bowler. I was now more than ever determined to do whatever I could to reunite Charlie and Hannah Chaplin.

Watching the films had given me an appetite at least for a bath bun and a cup of tea, so I indulged my appetite in a teashop as I considered my next activity. Whilst I considered that I had made good use of the afternoon I wondered what Holmes would make of my visit to the cinema? No matter, when I returned to Vaudeville House, I would meet the rest of my fellow guests and possibly learn even more from them. As the elderly waitress brought my tea, she enquired,

"Been to the flicks have you, love?"

I did not recognise the word flicks as she soon realised from my puzzled expression. She elucidated, "You know, the pictures. We calls 'em the flickers or the flicks. They've got old Charlie again this week. I think he's a real scream."

But her next words really did capture my, until then, wavering attention. She became all but conspiratorial in her tone, "They used to live just near here, you know, Charlie and his brother, Syd, and their poor mother. They often used to come in here and ask us for bread and dripping. She was a sweet soul was Hannah, quite ladylike, but full of fun. She had a wicked sense of humour. Used to take 'orf the other customers and she would have me in fits. Then she went a bit strange, suddenly very quiet where she had been full of life. Then they didn't come here no more and I heard that the boys had got jobs with Fred Karno, and poor Hannah had been taken off to the mad-house. Wicked, I reckon ..."

I waited, growing impatient for more information, then tried prompting, "You mean, you think she should not have been put in an asylum?"

"Hannah? Not on your life! When I say she became a little strange, I just mean strange for her – quiet, moody, tearful, but certainly not barmy, and she would never have hurt a fly, she wouldn't. Been quite well known on the halls in her day, you know. I remember when she was Lily Harley. It was that drunken husband of hers who dragged her down. Now *he* was the one who should have been in an asylum, deserting his lovely wife and two lovely boys."

I continued to try and draw her further, "I understand that he had been a big star himself, very clever song writer, too. I've also heard that he was very popular locally."

"Oh yes, popular with certain people. He even tried opening a public house, but he was his own best customer. He and his hangers-on soon put him out of business. But you know, Hannah and the boys never said a bad word about him. She ought to have been put in a home for saints, not lunatics. Still, she'll be all right now, eh? I mean with Charlie being a big film star, he'll look after his mother for sure."

One or two other patrons of the café, cabbies, navvies and other workmen soon joined in the conversation. They all remembered the Chaplins, and kindly too. One of them had memories of seeing Charlie at the Palace, Camberwell in Karno's *Mumming Birds* whilst another had seen Sydney and another clever comedian called Stan Laurel with another of Karno's companies. They all remembered Hannah, too, though only one of them remembered her from her days as Lily Harley. Everyone of them that I spoke to was adamant that she should not have been confined to an asylum.

One of them said, "If Hannah Chaplin was what you would call potty, blimey, they'd have had my old woman in a straight-jacket donkey's years ago!"

As I left that café, I got the distinct feeling that everyone within it felt that there was something sinister connected with the apprehension of Hannah by the authorities. When I reminded them that it had happened not once but several times, they felt that this fuelled their argument. "That they'd had to let her go before proves that she was right enough in the head."

To my relief Ada Foster appeared at the great trestle for an after-theatre snack. I had spent several hours first in the sitting room and later resting upon my bed, seemingly the only occupant of Vaudeville House, worrying that I should have taken my at least vague suspicion to Holmes rather than waiting until morning. Had I dropped a hint of my suspicion that could cause her to flee? Yes, I was relieved to see her.

Carl arrived from his nightly labours at Collins's and others came, that I had not as yet met. For example, I was introduced to Henry Hilton who had travelled back from the Bedford Music Hall, Camden Town, where he was appearing. He was, I soon discovered, a conjurer, and whilst he had returned from the theatre in street clothes, he had brought back a series of mysterious baskets and boxes, which it was soon evident contained living creatures. He was a man of perhaps forty years, but his demeanour and mannerisms were those of an older person. To see him pour himself a cup of coffee from the huge steaming communal pot was an experience. He displayed both his hands, and did it with a flourish, stopping short only of rolling his sleeves to the elbow. I half expected the coffee to sprout a flowering plant. In courtly style he passed Miss Foster a cup.

The next to arrive were a couple, Mr. and Mrs. Inglese who were evidently a very well-known juggling act. Ada explained to me *sotto voce* that they had a 'room on their own' which of course put them at the head of the class system of Vaudeville House. He told me to call him Rupert, in a manner which made me feel as if I should be honoured as if King George had suggested some familiarity. Later Carl explained to me that the Ingleses were 'on the number ones', which I assumed to mean that they worked only at the better class theatres. He confided to me,

"You must see their act some time, Barry, they are real class. They carry their own drapes and stage furnishings, including a standard lamp, which Rupert balances on the toe of his boot while he juggles with clubs. He makes a big entrance in a cloak while his wife plays upon the grand piano. He juggles with chairs, and even small tables where others use balls. Yet his big trick is with the smallest item; he throws a half crown up from his toe and catches it in his eye, like a monocle."

Mrs Inglese was a large, matronly woman with the air of a *grande dame*. She sat picking at a plate of ham and lettuce with a fork, rather as if feeling that it was expected of her. She confided to me,

"This is such a dear little place. Rupert and I have been staying here since we entered the profession, years ago. In those days we played places like Collins's and the Bedford, whereas now we are on the Moss Empires tour. We could stay at a good class hotel really, but this dear old place is more homely."

I decided to chance my arm, not for the first time that day, and asked her if they had ever been on the bill with Lily Harley. I took the chance because all else in the room were occupied with their various conversations and activities. Even so, I quickly wished that I had not mentioned Hannah Chaplin's stage name. Mrs. Inglese all but started, and her *pince nez* fell from her nose, dangling upon their silken cord.

However, she quickly recovered her aplomb and said, "She was before my time, Mr. Carstairs. Now, if you will excuse me, I must speak with Professor Hilton."

She abandoned her plate of ham and moved down the table. I realised that I had made a mistake, though just what its nature was I was not sure. Perhaps she was offended that I thought her old enough to have been in the business before the turn of the century? Or maybe she knew something about Hannah that would be of interest to Sherlock Holmes. But discretion being the better part of valour, I decided to leave things well alone.

The bed next to mine was occupied by Henri (Professor) Hilton. He did not snore, but I was kept awake by the scuttling noises from the mysterious boxes under his bed. Mark you, they were no longer mysterious to me because I had surprised him in the act of exercising what proved to be a group of fantailed pigeons. He implored me, "Shut the door quickly!" and I noted that he had closed all the windows. He mellowed as he caught the birds and returned them to their box. "Given half a chance it would be back to Trafalgar Square with the lot of them!" He laughed lightly at his own humour.

I decided, not for the first time that theatrical folk were more than a trifle strange.

Chapter Five

Comparing Notes with Sherlock Holmes

"Watson, my dear fellow, I have much to tell you, but first I feel that I should hear your own report. Let us comfortably seat ourselves, and partake of some excellent coffee."

Holmes had been awaiting my arrival as I walked into the entrance lobby of the Charing Cross Hotel. He steered me to a long sofa before which he caused a steaming pot of coffee, some rolls and butter and some digestive biscuits to be placed. We had the entrance lounge almost to ourselves for once, which was convenient.

"I have much to tell you, Holmes ..."

"In good time, Watson, rest and refresh yourself first. It is a splendid morning for the time of year, is it not?"

I found this manner of his a trifle irritating for I was bursting to tell him about Ada Foster, and other findings. However, it was typical of the mercurial Sherlock Holmes who on another day, and in another place, would be admonishing me for pausing for refreshment. He waved the hovering waiter aside and poured the coffee, then smiling enigmatically, he said, "Now, Watson, waste not a moment in giving me your findings."

I breathed hard at his irritating changes of mood, staged especially in this instance to vex me. I breathed hard, yet could not prevent the quick return of that feeling of suppressed excitement concerning what I would tell him.

"Holmes, I believe it possible … only possible, mark you … that I have actually found Hannah Chaplin."

I had his full attention as he turned to face me and said, "Tell me about this possibility."

Plunging in at the deep end, I began,

"Staying currently at Vaudeville House is a woman who reminds me of the later photograph of Hannah. Moreover, she had told me of a son who went to America to work for Mack Sennett, as indeed did Chaplin if you remember? She says that she had plans to join him in Hollywood."

"What is this woman's name?"

"She calls herself Ada Foster, but her real name is Ada Harding she claims, and gives her son's name as Robert Harding."

"Is she currently employed?"

"No, but she has expectations."

"You say she is a small, slightly built woman with grey hair?"

"Yes, with something in her face which makes me think of the way Hannah Chaplin might appear if those problems which had caused her expression of anxiety had been resolved."

"What colour are her eyes?"

I had only to pause momentarily to consider.

"Blue-grey."

By way of reply Holmes took the photograph of Hannah Chaplin from his inside breast pocket and laid it upon the long, low coffee table. He pointed at it with great drama as if in reply.

I said, "Being a photograph, the picture is in black and white."

Holmes shook his head, "Black, white and a number of shades of grey; yet see how dark her eyes appear."

"Might not the photographic process have translated them misleadingly?"

"No, indeed blue-grey would appear as very pale indeed, almost non-existent. I am afraid your Ada Foster is not Hannah Chaplin."

I suppose I must have muttered and grumbled a good deal, still perhaps with doubt in my tones, which caused him to say,

"Come, Watson, I believe we can confirm my doubts by consulting an expert. Finish your coffee, my dear fellow, we need to be moving."

Where he had at first tried to defer my excitement, he now proceeded to hurry me. He really could be exasperating. As we walked briskly down the Strand towards Fleet Street, I guessed that we were making for his variety agent, Charles Foster. As we walked, he said, "There is a coincidence which has I assume escaped your notice, Watson, concerning your lady's name?"

"Ada Foster?"

"Exactly, that surname is the same as that of the agent that we are going to visit."

I had to admit that this point had escaped me, but when we asked Charles Foster about Ada, he was very frank and open concerning his client.

"I gave her the name, Mr. Holmes, when we were in the act of signing a contract. Her usual theatrical name just did not seem suitable and I gave her my own name to save time and deliberation. She is at this moment residing at Vaudeville House in Brixton, but I am negotiating a part in a play for her. If this materialises, she will be able to move into slightly better accommodation."

Between them, Holmes and Foster convinced me that I had been wrong. We left him, as before, with a promise of confidentiality.

It was over a modest glass of ale in a hostelry that I gave Holmes the rest of my findings, which he fortunately found rather more impressive. His eyes opened wide at the information that I was able to give him concerning the Doughboys, especially that concerning the occasional hire of themselves and their vehicle for unusual purposes, and the possibility of their passing themselves off as ambulance men with the vehicle.

"Congratulations, Watson, you have indeed been busy. In fact, I am amazed that you found time to visit the cinema."

I started. "I do not believe that I mentioned visiting a cinema."

"There was no need for you to do so, my dear fellow, with your shilling ticket so neatly folded and inserted into the band of your hat. I approve of your choice of programme; it is good that you absorb as much as possible concerning our client."

"How do you know that I saw a Chaplin programme?"

"The name of the cinema is printed upon the ticket and I passed that establishment on my way back to Charing Cross by cab yesterday. Not even worthy of being called elementary, Watson."

There was little more for me to tell him, save some general impressions and of the rather pointed behaviour of Mrs. Inglese. Really I felt the time had arrived for Holmes to inform me of his own findings. He began casually enough, but as he proceeded a slight ring of excitement crept into his voice.

"I went to the address where we knew that the small member of the troupe lodged. I concealed myself among some bushes in the wild garden of a derelict property opposite. Eventually I was rewarded by the sight of the little fellow emerging from the house. He turned smartly (an expression that can also be applied to his appearance, save for his pallor) and walked briskly down the road. I followed him at a respectful distance and observed that he entered the precincts of a small park, where he met a woman, seemingly by arrangement, and they sat together in close converse upon a rustic bench. They appeared to be extremely friendly, just short of actual embrace."

I felt that it was perhaps my own turn to be unimpressed with some of his findings.

"So, the little fellow has a lady friend, and may even be what I believe is referred to in this day and age as walking out. I fail to see the significance, Holmes."

"Failing to see is one of your regular shortcomings, Watson."

"And the others?"

"Well, one of them is in coming to a conclusion before you have heard all of the evidence. Had you allowed me to elucidate further you would have heard the identity of the woman, an identity which even you might have considered significant."

I refused to ask further questions. His words had been hurtful, if not intriguing, and I awaited his continuance in his own time. Of course, continue in time, he did.

"The woman with whom the little fellow appeared to be on such close terms was that unfortunate one who serves as some sort of domestic for the Austins."

"You mean Gladys? I do not believe we were told any other name for her. She was as I remember rather slow on the uptake, practically an idiot."

"That was indeed the impression that she gave us when we met her, yet not that which I would have gained had I encountered her for the first time with her friend in the park. Her conversation appeared most lucid and rapid. Perhaps it suited her purpose to appear as one of life's unfortunates on the occasion of our visit, or conversely perhaps it was for the benefit of the Austins?"

"She had been close to Hannah according to what we were told."

"Exactly, Watson, and her connection with at least one of the Doughboys, allied to what you have learned of them makes me suspect that she acted as some sort of go-between."

"You mean between Hannah and the Doughboys?"

"Exactly. Maybe this was her way of escape, having tired of her long dull sojourn with the Austins. It could have been a way for her to depart from their house without their raising any sort of alarm, believing that she had been taken to the asylum."

"Why would this girl and the acrobats do this for her?"

"Either through friendship or for profit, Watson."

"Do you think she would have been in a financial position to reward them?"

"Probably not, but she may have had some jewellery or other objects of value that she had managed to hang onto from better times."

"Is there any way to confirm your suspicions, do you think?"

Holmes considered.

"If we were able to learn when the girl would again be away from the house, we could perhaps gain permission from the Austins to search her room during her absence. But in so doing we would have to take the chance concerning the complete lack of involvement of Ada and George Austin."

"Is it a chance worth taking?"

"I believe it is."

So it transpired that we watched the front of the Austin ménage that very afternoon to see if Gladys should leave the house. We fortunately had not long to wait and at about four o'clock she emerged, dressed in quite a respectable-looking coat. We gave her good time to get clear of the scene and then we rang the doorbell. It was George who answered the door to us, surprised but not in the least was he defensive.

"Mr. Holmes, Doctor, how nice to see you again. Do come in."

Ada Austin soon appeared and busied herself in preparing tea as we conversed with George. Holmes got straight to the business in hand, having evidently decided to cast aside all subtlety.

"Mr. Austin, we have reason to believe that your serving girl, Gladys, is not exactly as she seems."

Austin evidently misunderstood Holmes's meaning at first. "You mean that you had not realised that the poor girl is a few coppers short of a shilling?"

Holmes shook his head and explained, "On the contrary, my dear Austin, I believe that she wishes to give that impression, but is actually a reasonably intelligent woman."

He was more than a little surprised.

"But, Holmes, why on earth would she pose as being an idiot all this time?"

I felt that I might have the answer. "Perhaps she is very comfortable here, supported by you, and not expected to make more than a token effort toward being a servant."

Holmes nodded in agreement to my relief and Austin said, "I understand your point, Doctor, for indeed we ask very little of her on account of her mental infirmity."

Ada Austin joined us, carrying a tea tray which she set upon the table, saying, "The poor girl is out so I had to leave you to make the tea. She goes out most afternoons. I like her to get the air, poor thing."

It was George who explained to her that which he had heard from us. Holmes completed the story, telling of his suspicions concerning her connection with the Doughboys. The story was a little hard to swallow for both of them, but I could see that they suspected that Holmes could be right.

At length Ada asked, "How can we help you in confirming your suspicions, Mr. Holmes?"

My friend explained.

"I believe that a search of her room might reveal some object, or objects of value, which Hannah Chaplin might have given her in return for aiding her escape."

His last word seemed to upset Ada.

"Escape? Why should poor Hannah want to escape from us? We always treated her as a friend, despite her eccentricities. She never had to go anywhere alone, and she had all she needed here. The only alternative would have been a return to the asylum, which is what we believed had happened."

Holmes spoke to her gently.

"Mrs. Austin, I know that you and your husband did for her all that you could. But it is my theory that her mental illness had all but lifted from her mind. She had waited so long for her sons to take her away to the Americas that she had lost patience and had concocted some sort of plan to take up fresh identity and make her own way to the New World."

The Austins accompanied us as we searched Gladys's room for any sort of sign that might confirm Holmes's suspicions. He found that which he was looking for in a dressing table drawer in the shape of a trinket box. He opened it to reveal a number of cheap pieces of jewellery of the kind that a servant girl might be expected to own. But there underneath some others was a brooch in the form of a flying horse composed of small glittering stones.

Austin peered at it. "Paste, I suppose, Holmes?"

Having taken his lens to the object, my friend said, "No, the diamonds are real enough, and there are some at the base describing the letters 'LH'."

He did not need to explain the significance of these letters.

"By George, Lily Harley!" I felt that one of us needed to say this.

Holmes explained, "There may have been others, by now either sold or pawned to bribe the acrobats to perform that service."

He returned the piece to its place underneath the examples of glass rubies and diamante.

He said, "I think we should confront the girl with that which we believe when she returns."

George Austin asked, rather anxiously, "Does this mean that you will need to call upon the police?"

Holmes shook his head.

"I believe not. I feel that their involvement might lead to the discovery of Hannah and her return to an asylum. I would like to find her but only in order to avoid that course. But we shall have to see what Gladys has to say for herself when she returns."

We had to wait for two hours for Gladys to make her reappearance at the Austin house, during which time Holmes amazed me with the way in which he made great efforts to entertain George and Ada – as if he were their host rather than the reverse being so. He seemed to feel a need to charm them with witty conversation and stories of cases in which we had been involved. I began to think that it should have been he rather than I who should have made written accounts of these for posterity. But then Sherlock Holmes had always been a splendid raconteur, even if he seldom used this all but theatrical talent. By the time he had related the strange events that had occurred at Stoke Moran and of the adventure of the Musgrave ritual, they were, I felt, his friends for life.

Ada had gone to prepare yet another pot of tea when footfalls were heard upon the drive. George leapt up to see if it was Gladys returning. Holmes took this opportunity to say to me quietly, "In case you have wondered at my histrionics, Watson, their reason was to secure them as allies rather than just tolerant of our activities."

The front door opened and George's voice could be heard.

"Gladys, pray hurry, we have visitors and they wish to speak with you. It is Sherlock Holmes and Dr. Watson, whom you have already met."

He brought her into the sitting room minus her top coat. When she saw us, she threw us some sort of clumsy curtsey. If Holmes was right concerning her dual personality, she had very quickly resumed playing the part of an idiot serving girl. Ada returned with the tea and spoke, not unkindly, to Gladys.

"Where have you been, my dear, we were beginning to become worried about you."

The girl fumbled some words, "Out ... just out."

George was a little more stern of manner, saying, "Of course you have been out, but you must have been somewhere during the past two hours, Gladys?"

She was defensive. "Walking ... been for a walk."

At this point Holmes decided to take over the situation. He gestured to a chair in which he wished her to sit. She glanced at George and Ada in turn, then when they had both nodded, she sat down. He spoke kindly to her as if dealing with a frightened animal.

"Gladys, you have been for a walk, but you did not walk all the time, did you? You must surely have stopped to rest?"

"Yes ... stopped to rest."

"Did you talk with anyone?"

"No ... not allowed to talk ..."

Ada interjected. "That is right. I have always told her to talk to no one, especially strange men."

Sherlock Holmes and the Charlie Chaplin Affair

Holmes nodded to Ada, smiled and then resumed questioning Gladys.

"But then the little fellow is not a strange man, is he, Gladys, because you know him well. Did you sit with him upon the rustic bench in the park as before?"

She did not reply, simply looking shocked as Holmes continued.

"Did you tell him about the brooch with the diamonds, the one that Hannah used to wear?"

She started, sat up straight, her whole manner changing with the character of the vacant-faced woman falling away from her. She was no longer slack-mouthed as she was shocked into her reply.

"It is mine, Hannah gave it to me. You are not to say that I stole it from her! Has Hannah said that I stole it?"

Holmes calmed her.

"Come, Gladys, no one is accusing you of stealing. So, Hannah gave it to you. Did she give you other things, too, for you perhaps to sell for her so that you could pay the little fellow, who is I believe your friend, and his colleagues to pretend to be ambulance men and help her to leave here?"

She gave up all pretence of playing the simpleton as she replied in a quite well-spoken voice.

"There is only one way you could know all this. You have found Hannah. In which case she will have told you that she gave me the brooch. I did nothing wrong, she told me that if she had to stay here much longer, Mr. and Mrs. Austin would get tired of keeping her and she would be taken away to the asylum. Well, I have been in an asylum, and it is terrible to have to live there, so I wanted to help her. She wanted to join her son in America, but had given up hope of him coming here to get her."

Everything that she said confirmed all that we had constructed by investigation and deduction. But now Holmes needed her co-operation rather than her defensiveness.

He said, "Gladys, as you must know Hannah's son, Charles, did in fact arrive to take her back with him to

America, but alas he arrived too late, after these events had occurred. Why did you not tell him what you have told me?"

She said, "I was frightened of getting into trouble, which for me could only have ended in the asylum. What is more, even if that didn't happen, Mr. and Mrs. Austin would undoubtedly have told me to go, and where would I have gone?"

Holmes was at his most reassuring.

"Gladys, Mr. and Mrs. Austin have assured me that they would like you to stay, upon terms that they will doubtless negotiate with you. Moreover, it is not my intention to do anything that might compromise you in any way. I am interested only in finding Hannah, in order to assist her to do the very thing which she herself wishes to do – to join her sons, Charles and Sydney, in America. All I ask of you is that you help me to find her so that I might help her. Do you, or your friends, the Doughboys, have any knowledge concerning her present whereabouts?"

Reassured, she sat forward in her chair, the relief clear in her voice. "No, sir, but I will help you in any way I can. The last I heard was that she had been put down at Victoria Station from the van. She had promised to write, but I suppose she decided that it would be unwise to do so for the present?"

Other questions followed from Holmes, but her answers only led to the same few facts that had already been established. Holmes summed up by making a few financial enquiries.

"How much money did you raise from the jewellery?"

"About a hundred pounds altogether. She paid the Doughboys twenty-five pounds, and she gave me the brooch which I had admired before."

"So, she arrived at Victoria with about seventy-five pounds in her purse. Not a huge sum, but enough for her to be able to live comfortably enough for quite a few weeks if she was careful. We know her goal was to travel to America, but of her immediate plans we know nothing. She must have had some sort of short-term ambition in mind. She did not mention anything of this?"

"No, sir, she kept saying that she felt sure she could earn a living on her own. I wondered if she meant to return to the stage, but I can't quite picture that happening."

We left the Austins and Gladys wiser regarding Hannah Chaplin than they had been when we had arrived at their home. The kindly couple reassured us regarding Gladys's future as we departed to find a cab.

Our first destination was Vaudeville House where I collected the few pieces of clothing that I had left there in the Gladstone bag. I made my apologies to the landlady, thrusting some money into her hands and saying, "A part has been offered to me, but I have to go to Manchester for it."

She accepted this in the matter-of-fact style of a theatrical landlady. So, I was able to slip away from my short theatrical career as a character actor. Our next stop was at my home in Finchley where Holmes refused my invitation to a meal, saying, "I have work to do, Watson, but all you need to do is pack some fresh linen for perhaps a week away from home."

"Where are we going?"

"I will answer that question when I meet you under the clock tomorrow morning at Victoria station. Half past nine will be a suitable time, but don't be late as we have a train to catch on the hour."

Chapter Six

'London by the Sea'

London's Victoria station has always fascinated me, for unlike the other big main railway depots, it is devoted almost entirely to transporting people to the coast for purposes of enjoyment. At certain times of the year the holidaymakers greatly outnumber those who work in the offices and factories with which they commute upon a daily basis. In consequence this particular station has an air of optimism and suppressed excitement. The shops near the station may not sell buckets and spades or 'kiss me quick' hats, but they are not those of dull everyday commerce.

"Watson, I see you are punctual for once and looking alert, which is a good sign. We just have time to repair to the refreshment room."

As the waitress in her spotless lace apron and cap brought us some coffee, I glanced around the huge refreshment hall with its marble-topped tables at which sat cheery Cockney family parties, in brighter versions of 'Sunday best', their children in their clean white collars and pinafores, demanding drinks and cakes and asking endless questions. Indeed, Holmes and I must have stood out from the mass for once in our sober attire. I took a sip of coffee and then demanded that which I felt I had the right to know.

"Exactly where, Holmes, are we going?"

"I will let you work out the answer to that question for yourself, Watson. If you were Hannah Chaplin, and you had demanded to be dropped off here, where would you be likely to travel?"

"Perhaps Guildford or Haywards Heath, or possibly Redhill."

"Why would you choose one of three such places?"

"Well, remembering my background as an invalid I would choose somewhere quiet."

"My dear Watson, I suppose you could be right, though my own feelings are that she would not be looking to hide away."

"Why not, pray?"

"Well to begin with you would be running away from years of seclusion and would also be seeking to earn some sort of livelihood. The seventy-five pounds will not last forever."

I shrugged and suggested that he inform me of his own suspicions as to her destination. By way of answer he pushed across the table a first-class ticket for Brighton, saying, "You will need that Watson, if you are to accompany me."

Brighton, then as now was a large seaside resort with a considerable resident population which probably doubled during the summer months. It had so much to offer from the stately Pavilion of King George IV and the bustling antique shops of The Lanes, to the pleasure domes and piers, theatres, dance halls, funfairs, and even the oldest and largest aquarium in Britain. There was also a shopping area to rival those of Oxford and Regent Streets and a racecourse, which brought to the town those who followed the sport of kings. It had so many amenities that it had become known as 'London by the Sea', and of course that great and rolling ocean was the cherry on the cake. People had been going to Brighton to bathe in its cooling channel waters and to breathe in its bracing salt air for perhaps a century and a half, since the fishing village of Brighthelmstone had been converted into a playground for rich and poor alike. It was still the same, for if you were rich you stayed at The Grand or The Metropole; if less prosperous you stayed at a boarding house for a week, but if you were poor or nearly so, you took a day trip to

Brighton from Victoria. All of this ran through my mind and eventually I asked, "What, then, do you think she would have done in Brighton in order to better her fortunes – sold rock upon the promenade or become a shop assistant at Wades?"

He blanched slightly at my rare irony and replied,

"During the season, Watson, there are fully a dozen places of theatrical entertainment in Brighton. These range from an elaborate variety theatre and two or three smaller ones, to several legitimate houses, a concert party or two and theatres at the end of each pier. It would be the perfect place for Hannah to reside, and find some sort of theatrical employment. Moreover, she would be less likely to be recognised or identified, assuming that she changed her stage name."

There was logic in his words, but as the Surrey countryside gave way for that of the Sussex Downs, I began to wonder if we were not upon a wild goose chase. At Brighton station I breathed the good salt air and decided that I would go along with Holmes's nose for these things, if only because my constitution would be better for a seaside break.

We put up at a hotel which was not as grand as those that I have mentioned, yet was rather more comfortable than the smaller ones might have been. It was right on the seafront which before the day was out became awash with seawater hurled against the cliff which had long formed the foundation for the promenade itself. To the east the natural cliffs were still being eroded by such treatment from the wild sea, yet to the west the sea had always been calmer, making Hove and Portslade more tranquil. We braved the gale and well-muffled, stepped out onto the promenade to survey the scene and discuss our first moves.

We gazed down to the beach, so far below the promenade that a second one, whilst less ambitious, had been built at a halfway height. We descended to this lesser thoroughfare by means of some steps, a great many of them. I could see that Holmes enjoyed the spray on his face as much as I did as we glanced to the beach itself. The rock stalls were closed but a lone photographer braved the weather to very poor result.

However, his appearance seemed to spark some thought in Holmes's fertile mind which he translated for me at dinner at The Salisbury.

"Watson, if you were a thespian or vaudeville artiste and had been out of the business for many years, what would be your first port of call when finding yourself in completely fresh territory?"

I thought carefully before replying.

"I would imagine some sort of costume, some cosmetics, things of that kind."

He nodded sagely.

"Your answer shows great practicality, Watson, but let us assume for just a moment that the artiste had such things carefully preserved from happier times. What else would be essential, in order that you could make a fresh beginning?"

I could not think of any one specific necessity.

He said, "Photographs, Watson, professional portraits, or at least one such. The thought occurred to me when we watched the unfortunate street photographer upon that windswept beach. In Brighton there will be many photographers, yet I feel sure that there will be just one or two who specialise in theatrical work. I believe we should seek these out upon the morrow."

In a town the size of Brighton there are possibly a hundred or so photographers, not counting itinerants who ply their trade upon the seafront. I wondered just how Holmes would discover which of these specialised in theatrical work. He did so in the most direct method when he walked into the office of one of the local newspapers, *The Evening Argus*. There in the reception area were a number of copies of the journal. Holmes picked up two of them and handed one to me, saying, "Come, Watson, I do not need to tell you what to look for."

I turned to the classified columns and found 'Photographers', all but a column of them. Three of these were of interest: Geo. White, Commercial and Theatrical Photograph; Nunn and Sons, Theatre and Family Portraits and Alexander, Photographer to the Stars and Gentry. I could see that Holmes had circled with pencil the same three advertisements that had caught my own eye. He dropped sixpence upon the counter when an office boy arrived to attend us.

Holmes enquired of him, "My friend is an actor, wishing to find a theatrical photographer to make some professional portraits. There are three such men listed among your advertisements. Which would you recommend?"

The lad was thoughtful, and then when he spoke he demonstrated that his intellect was above average.

"Well, sir, it would depend. The three of them are good photographers, but if your friend has to watch his finances, I would recommend Mr. Nunn. We publish quite a lot of his work in our paper, mostly of music hall artistes when they appear locally. But if your friend wanted real quality without counting the cost, he would want to go to Alexander."

Holmes nodded wisely, and I enquired, "How about this George White?"

"George is good too, and not expensive, but he is a bit of a plodder. Gets a bit of work through having been in the business himself. A lot of artistes remember him from the old days and patronise him for that reason."

I noticed that Holmes slipped the youth a half crown as he turned to leave and as we stepped out onto the street, he said, "What a bright lad, Watson, although it remains to be seen if his advice will bear fruit, yet one must admire his train of thought and practicality."

We took ourselves to the address in London Road which the advertisement indicated. A rather seedy-looking double-fronted shop housed Mr. White's enterprise, which we entered to find a rather dyspeptic-looking middle-aged man at a desk, writing a letter upon a typewriting machine. At the rear, through a partly opened drape, we could see a rather large old-style camera on a tripod and a stool before a painted backcloth of a woodland glade. Obviously Mr. White was not being overwhelmed with clients. He looked up brightly as we entered.

"Good morning, gentlemen, double act are you, comic and feed? I've got a lovely street scene that would do you a treat."

As I began a muttered protestation, Holmes managed to neatly kick me in the ankle and drown the sound of my voice with a stentorian address.

"Exactly so, Bedlow and Barker, but I am not sure that it is a street scene that we need."

White picked up an all but gigantic photograph album and passed it to us, saying, "Take a look at some examples of my work. All the backdrops that I have you will find among those portraits."

Holmes spread the album upon his lap as he sat in a wicker chair, opening the pages and studying each photograph with interest. I leaned over to see them as best I could. Each picture had a name written beneath it, along with a few details such as the date upon which the sitting had occurred and the address of the sitter. There was a conjurer, Holden, a living marionette act, singers, comedians in full comic make-up and one or two of the portraits struck chords in my memory. We were supposed to be looking for a suitable backdrop, but I knew that Holmes was seeking a likeness that could conceivably be that of Hannah.

I believe that I spotted her first. There was a picture of a middle-aged woman in a Pierrot costume. Despite the ruffle and voluminous attire, I could see the striking dark eyes, slightly prominent teeth and high cheekbones of the lady we were seeking. I knew that I did not need to draw Holmes's attention to the picture, but I did so in what I considered to be a subtle way of doing so without placing all our cards upon the table. I pointed to the portrait and said, "Ah, now there is a very fine backdrop. Looks like the interior of a stately home. I like the painted candelabra overhead."

I memorised the name and address: Ella Queen, c/o Mrs Styles, 42 Green Dragon Street. There was a date early in 1919, which fitted in with the disappearance of Hannah Chaplin. Holmes indicated the picture and said to White, "Yes, this is the background that would suit us best. I recognise an old friend of ours, too, Ella Queen."

George White studied the portrait with pride.

"A good picture, eh? Miss Queen came in for it a couple of years ago. Nice lady and although I had never met her before she reminded me of Lily Harley. Something about the bone structure of the face. Poor old Lily, I heard she was in a mental home: believes she is Charlie Chaplin's mother!"

I dared to ask a question, "Had she just arrived in Brighton?"

"So she said, told me she had lost all her clothes and props in a fire, even her professional pictures. Needed to replace everything. Maybe it was just a hard luck story, but I let her have the sitting at a reduced price. Well, if she was digging in Green Dragon Street, she can't have been very wealthy. She asked me if I knew of any show that she might get into, and I suggested she should go and see Jack Shepherd. He's got the best concert party in Brighton, and he often uses older lady singers and comediennes. Hang on, and I'll sort out that palace scene ..."

As he went to his little stage and busied himself with ropes and pulleys, I glanced at Holmes almost in desperation. I had thought that having gained this valuable lead he would wish to wash his hands of Bedlow and Barker, but he continued to play his role as one of a pair of comedic actors. Then when White had fixed the scene, he enquired of Holmes, "I take it you are Mr. Bedlow?"

"That is so."

"Thought so, the straight man usually gets first billing."

Holmes was intrigued, "What made you so sure that I was the foil?"

White chuckled, "You are made for the part – tall, slim, with a very decisive manner. Your friend now, Mr. Barker, he is obviously a born comic with that droopy moustache and sadness of expression."

I said nothing to this indignity, little aware that I would soon suffer another. White placed Holmes centre stage and enquired, "Do you want to make up or change? I notice you have brought no costumes. Shall I lend you something?"

Holmes explained that we were wearing our professional clothing and that we worked without make up. White nodded with comprehension.

"You work in the new casual style, eh? No red noses or funny clobber. Well, I suggest that you give me some idea of how you begin your act. Assume that the band have played *Ta-ra-ra Boom-de-ay*. I'm using these new fast plates, so you don't need to stand still."

I saw the gleam of mischief in Holmes's eyes as he stood at the centre of the little platform.

He said, "I start us off by reciting a monologue and Mr. Barker interrupts me with some witty sayings."

As Holmes started to recite *Gunga Din*, I racked my brains for some comic remark that I might have heard or read. I stepped forward and said, "I say, five people were caught out in a field without an umbrella, yet none of them got wet."

Holmes was relentless.

"How was it that none of them got wet?"

I played my trump card.

"It wasn't raining!"

Holmes snapped back, "Don't interrupt. I'm reciting *Gunga Din*."

To my astonishment, White came out from under his black cloth and was shaking with laughter.

"Jolly good! That's one good picture, I'm sure. Now let's try another."

The few minutes that passed were for me a nightmare of half-remembered childish jokes. Holmes played up as if born to be a comedian's straight man.

When this terrible ordeal was over, White said, "I'll have them ready tomorrow, gentlemen, but I wonder if I could ask you for a deposit. Shall we say a pound? It is usual practice."

Holmes insisted upon paying for the whole operation saying that it might be a while before we would call again. The photographer was happy with this and shook hands with us in turn.

'London by the Sea'

"No matter when. I'm sure you will be happy with the pictures, and let me compliment you on your style. Unusual, but I'm sure you will succeed."

After we had left the shop I rounded upon Holmes, asking him, "Was it really necessary for you to put us through that charade when we had gained more information than we had dreamed possible?"

Holmes chuckled, "I did not wish to mark White's card concerning our real activities. What better than that he should believe us to be a comedic vaudeville team?"

My equanimity gradually restored itself as I considered what had fallen from the sky without our having to have fired a shot – save the ridicule to which I had been subjected. I said, with some excitement, "I felt sure that you would be as convinced as I that the photograph was of Hannah, but White's words concerning her likeness to Lily Harley was surely confirmation?"

"Agreed, Watson, and we must take care that the nearer we move toward our goal the more care we must take in disguising our intentions. Our bird is sensitive and flighty and will depart at the slightest sign of pursuit. We will continue to tread softly on our visit to the house in Green Dragon Street."

As it happened that thoroughfare proved to be a side street near to the arches beneath Brighton Station. The Green Dragon public house on the corner was the obvious reason for the street's name. We knocked at the door of a tiny terrace house which was number 42, and that door was opened by an elderly lady wearing the man's cap and huge carpet slippers of her kind.

"Yes, I am Mrs. Styles. As you say, Ella Queen stayed with me a couple of years ago. She did the summer season with Jack Shepherd's concert party down on the front. She left at the end of the season same as the others. Don't tell me she owes you money because she always paid me on the dot. Nice woman."

Holmes explained that he wanted to inform her of something which was to her advantage, which was true. The landlady mellowed.

"Why don't you ask them down at the concert party if they know where she went. She never told me and I don't stick my nose into other folk's affairs."

We walked down the Queen's Road, past the Victorian clock tower with its mosaic Royal portraits and down the length of West Street to the seafront. It was a pleasing downhill walk, despite its distance, and it gave us a chance to converse concerning our next move.

"The cast of the concert party may change each season, Watson, but if we ask Mr. Shepherd he may be of help."

Jack Shepherd's concert party proved to be housed in a shed of a theatre, *al fresco*, with the seating being inside a three-sided low wooden fence. The little stage backed on to the beach and faced the promenade where a crowd of people were leaning over to get a free view of the show. It was all but time for the matinée and so we paid our shillings and sat down within the enclosure. After a while a pianist, in a blue blazer and white trousers, entered to take his seat upon the stool. He played a rousing overture, which he followed with the opening chorus which introduced the six performers, three men and three women. All wore blue blazers, the men with white trousers and the women in white pleated skirts. The company consisted of a young woman with a roughish manner (soubrette), a hefty elderly man with a deep voice (baritone), a stout elderly woman with an amusing style (comedienne), a tall well-built young man with expressive eyes and a cheeky smile (comedian), a flaxen-haired lady with a regal air (soprano) and a slim young man who moved well as he joined the chorus (singer/dancer). As the six of them reached the climax of their opening chorus, an elderly man, also in blazer and white trousers stepped out in front of them and waved to the crowd. There were not too many paying patrons, but they cheered and shouted "Good old Jack", so we knew that this was the eminent and elegant Mr. Jack Shepherd. As the company waved and made their exits, he introduced the first item, a song by the soubrette which was rousing, amusing and got the show off to a good start. As she finished, she in her turn introduced the artiste who followed her, "Mr. Harry Sergeant."

We will not bore the reader with a recitation of the bright little show which took place – songs, sketches, dances and comic monologues – yet I must mention that I found Mr. Sergeant quite the most amusing fellow that I had seen upon the stage. He said amusing things, he sang songs – which were almost but not quite risqué, – above all he had one of those smiles which started in a small way and built up to the biggest open grin imaginable. He cajoled the old ladies in the audience by saying, "I don't care what I say, lady, do I, eh?"

I turned to Holmes and asked, "I wonder why this fellow Sergeant is not starring at one of the big music halls?"

He was also impressed, saying, "Given time, Watson, I feel sure that he will."

During the interval a collection was made from the people who were watching from beyond the fence. This job also went to Sergeant who brandished a small black bag, even climbing the hundred or so stairs. After the performance it was Harry Sergeant who we first asked concerning Ella Queen.

He said, "I wasn't with the show that year, I was still at St Dunstan's, blind as a bat I was from being too near when a German shell went off. Mind you, I soon got my sight back and now I'll do anything for the blind. Know what it's like, see."

We congratulated him on his performance and he enjoyed our praise, saying, "I've got big plans, I'm going into variety at the end of this season, got a new name and all – Max Miller, how does that sound?"

Holmes remarked shrewdly that the name would look good on the bills, then requested that we be allowed to speak with Jack Shepherd. The white-haired impresario was polite but could not help us a great deal.

"She was a good performer despite her age ... there is many a good tune played upon an old fiddle ... I would have rebooked her for the following season but she seemed anxious to be on her way. Didn't say so, but it was just a feeling that I got."

Shepherd allowed us to ask the other performers but they all said she was a pleasant woman but with a certain reserve. The baritone, Charles Mellowman, told us,

"She was good for this show because she had a large repertoire. She used to do all of Lily Harley's numbers, many that Marie Lloyd made famous, and she would even put on a tailcoat and sing *Burlington Bertie*. I have an idea that she planned to go to Worthing for the pantomime season."

It was not too late even then for us to visit the public library which was housed in the beautiful Pavilion. Holmes not only knew his way there but quickly led me to the reading room where reference facilities were available. When I expressed some mild surprise at this, he reminded me that he lived at Fowlhaven, which was but a few miles from where we stood.

"I am merely retired from active professional work, Watson. This does not mean that I have ceased to take an interest in what happens around me. I have frequently used this library for research. I am known here as Mr. Winter."

The lady who we dealt with smiled at Holmes and indeed called him by that name. He requested a file of *The Worthing Gazette* covering December 1919 and January 1920. The bound issues for the years 1919 and 1920 shortly arrived by way of a lift from the floor below, rather as the hot meals are dispatched from a hotel kitchen. We took a volume each to a table, and I was struck with their similarity to those books in which sample sheets of wallpaper are bound.

I was the first to find an advertisement for a pantomime: *Cinderella*, which would open on Boxing Day, 1920. Sure enough, the cast included 'Ella Queen as Baroness Hardup'.

I said, "Holmes, I believe you might find a critique for the pantomime in the first issue in your volume. It was at the Empress Theatre."

My friend read aloud a paragraph which included mention of Hannah:

'London by the Sea'

"The Baroness was played with style and comicality by Miss Ella Queen who is, I believe, new to Empress audiences. Indeed, when she had the opportunity in the ballroom scene to indulge in a solo performance, she quite lifted the show with her music hall impersonations of Marie Lloyd, Ella Shields and Lily Harley. The last-named impersonation was all but uncanny as elders in the audience would confirm."

By taking an omnibus along the coastal road we were able that very evening to journey to Worthing, less than ten miles from Brighton and attend a performance at the Empress Theatre. That Shaw's *Candida* attracted an almost capacity house at a resort theatre shows how very different Worthing is from Brighton. During one of the intervals we were able to contact the Manager of the theatre, a Mr. Barclay, who was as helpful as he was able to be to us in our pursuit of Hannah Chaplin.

"Ella Queen? Why yes, she was here the Christmas before last in the pantomime. Good performer, but very quiet, kept herself to herself. Where the others stayed in pro digs for instance, she stayed at the Desmond, which is a small hotel on the front. I believe I heard that she was going to Southampton when the panto closed, though just why I don't know."

The Desmond proved to be a small but smart-looking establishment where the bar was open to non-residents. We patronised it in a casual manner, though Holmes did enquire of the barmaid concerning Ella Queen. She was very forthcoming, saying, "Oh yes, my love, she stayed here while she was in the pantomime. Used to come in here straight from the theatre and I would get her a half bottle of wine and a chicken sandwich. Your long-lost cousin, eh? I should have a word with them at the desk, she might have left an address. All I know is that she once said something about going to Southampton."

Ella Queen had left no forwarding address, but we had heard mention of Southampton as her possible destination from two sources – the barmaid at the Desmond Hotel and the Manager at the Empress Theatre. Holmes studied his hunter.

"Fortunately, the station is near and we have just time to catch the last train to Brighton."

That train took us through Lancing, Shoreham, Fishersgate, Portslade and Hove. At Brighton station we managed to get a cab down to our hotel where we took coffee in the lounge prior to retiring. We discussed what we had learned and agreed that we had covered much ground in just a few hours.

I enquired, "Shall you be going to Southampton?"

There was an ironic touch to his voice as he replied, "Certainly, Watson, and so will you, for the time fast nears when we must travel from there to New York, with or without Hannah Chaplin."

Chapter Seven

Sherlock Holmes in Hollywood

"There she is at last, Watson!"

We were on the deck of the *Olympic* which was entering New York Harbour. Holmes and I had taken up the tickets which Chaplin had left for us after arriving in Southampton several days in advance of the departure that we might have a last minute attempt to trace Hannah Chaplin, or Ella Queen as she had more lately been known. We thought to have picked up the trail several times, only on each occasion to have our hopes dashed. I knew that Holmes, whilst keeping to his arrangement with Chaplin, could find little pleasure in making this long trip to report failure. I must admit that I felt a certain amount of guilt, feeling that my own anticipation of a visit to the United States may have coloured my friend's decision to follow the plan. He could after all have wired Chaplin that we were not coming and I believe he would have preferred to do so. But my heart all but missed a beat when he spoke the words.

I gasped the enquiry, "You have spotted Hannah?"

"No, Watson, the 'Lady with the Light', the Statue of Liberty. A magnificent sight, is she not?"

My annoyance at my own foolish interpretation of his words soon passed in the excitement of disembarkation. We were met by a Mr. Stark who told us that he was Chaplin's New York representative and he conveyed us by cab to a splendid hotel, The Majestic where we were to spend the night prior to entraining for California. These were Chaplin's orders to Stark after an exchange of wires. I felt sad to think that his hopes, however slight of our having brought Hannah with us, had been dashed at the end of a telegraph wire.

We had very little time to take in the sights of New York, preferring anyway to partake of a splendid meal at the hotel. I knew not what a Porterhouse steak might be but can assure the reader that I was happy to have taken a chance with that choice and that it was far from the last time that I enjoyed the dish. It was served with sauté potatoes and cabbage. I followed this by a dish called Pie à la mode, which turned out to be an enormous portion of ice cream served with a fruit pie slice. The wine left quite a lot to be desired, however, and Holmes, although he enjoyed the trout that he had ordered, complained at the quantity that he was obliged to leave upon his plate.

Later over coffee we gave Mr. Stark some account of our adventures in following the trail of Hannah Chaplin.

He was impressed, saying, "Maybe Charlie was wrong to insist that you leave England at a specific time rather than leave it to you to give up the chase when there was no more clue left."

Holmes was enigmatic as he replied,

"My dear Stark, I am not certain that we had not reached such a situation."

"You mean to say that the great Sherlock Holmes had been defeated by a lady where emperors of crime have failed?"

Holmes's eyes narrowed but he showed no other sign of annoyance as he replied,

"Not quite, Stark, but you know how difficult it is to pick up the scent again when the fox has leapt over water."

It was not until we were safely installed upon the California-bound train that I thought to question Holmes concerning this remark.

He said, "Watson, I believe that Hannah did indeed cross the water – not a ditch, or stream or even just a river, but a mighty ocean; the Atlantic!"

I whistled, "You mean you think she sailed to America?"

"Everything seems to point to it, Watson. We know her goal was to join her son in California. All that stood between her and that goal back in 1920 would have been the price of her passage. As far as I can see she might well have gained enough from several months of hard work."

I considered, "She might have saved enough to go steerage, I suppose?"

It was a wonderful experience that long train journey, the longest I had ever undertaken unless you consider aged steam engines in India. There, of course, the journey had been interrupted by raiding parties. Here the train was free to make its way first to Washington where many more persons entrained, through the Deep South and the Midwest, until we made our way over the Great Plains and endless desert.

Sherlock Holmes spent most of his time in the club car whilst I rejoiced in a seat upon the observation platform. I enjoyed the sights of vast herds of cattle, wild antelope and in places, vast seas of wheat. Earlier I had marvelled at the tobacco and cotton where labourers worked tirelessly.

Indeed, I can heartily recommend a New York to California rail journey as a great introduction to that wonderful collection of what seem for all the world like a series of different countries – the United States of America.

On the final day of our journey we had reached a stop, which I understood to be in the very centre of the Mojave desert. I had managed to tempt Holmes out on to the observation platform at the back of the train. We were standing suddenly aware that there was nothing to be seen but sand, scrub, cactus and rocks as far as the eye could see in any direction. I admit this made me realise our own small part in Nature's plans. There we were, just the two of us standing upon the platform when the train came to a slow shuddering halt. The guard came out onto the platform and said, making a suggestion, "We stop here for twenty minutes, gentlemen, so you have just time to stretch your legs and take a looksee if you are inclined to do so?"

We thanked him for this information and decided to take him up on this suggestion. He lowered some steps and we descended onto the sand beside the railroad track. We had lit our pipes and had wandered perhaps a hundred yards from the train when I suddenly noticed that the guard had pulled up the steps. Holmes noticed this too and additionally mentioned that we were the only passengers to take advantage of this chance to descend. Moreover, the guard had our luggage out on the step and this seemed also singular.

But this was just the appetiser to what was about to happen. I assumed that the guard had taken leave of his senses when he threw our luggage down on to the track. He laughed hugely as we started hastily for the platform. Then he pulled the cord which operated the whistle which signalled the train to depart.

There was no possibility that we could catch up with the moving train, though we did get close enough to hear him shout, "Enjoy your walk, gentlemen."

As the train gradually became smaller until it was a dot on the horizon, I broke the shocked silence which we had both observed.

"What do you make of that, Holmes? Is the fellow potty or what?"

He laughed bitterly.

"Far from it I would say, Watson. There is rather more to it than that. At this moment I can only deduce that he has been bribed by someone with a warped sense of humour to put us in this position. Just who or why I cannot as yet imagine. Moreover, the guard must realise that retribution will follow when we eventually reach our destination. He seems not to care about that."

I said, bitterly, "You believe then that we can reach Los Angeles and will not die of starvation or heat here in the desert?"

"Oh, come, Watson, we have only to follow the railway track. We are on the last lap of our journey, so if we walk for perhaps a day, we should reach the outskirts of civilisation."

On reflection I should have been heartened by his words, yet I admit that at the time I had no joy in the thought of walking for a day through the desert, carrying my luggage!

"Could we not wait for the next train?"

"You may, if you want to wait for two days and then risk it not stopping for you. I shall start walking very shortly."

I considered his words, which as always were wise. We would scarcely die of hunger or thirst within twenty-four hours, and so our survival was not in doubt if we started walking. If we did not there could be some risk involved. We finished our pipes and then picked up our bags and started to follow the tracks. We walked for perhaps two hours before we stopped for a rest. By that time our condition was far from comfortable with the noonday sun taking its toll of us. Holmes decreed that we should make a shelter with our canes and greatcoats that we might enjoy shade for the worst part of the day.

"We will take a *siesta*, Watson, then we will redouble our efforts in the cool of the evening."

When I awoke it was with an almighty thirst. Holmes was standing searching the far distance with shaded eyes. He spoke to me without looking round, evidently his acute hearing having told him that I was awake.

"What do you make of the cloud on the horizon, Watson?"

I followed his gaze. There did seem to be a small distant cloud of dust.

I suggested, "A sandstorm?"

He shook his head.

"I do not think so, Watson, it is somewhat confined for such a phenomena. I fancy it is a group of men on horses. It may be that our troubles are over."

However, he would scarcely repeat this opinion within a few minutes, for the riders were to prove far from friendly. As soon as we could clearly see them, they appeared to be a group of Mexicans, but far from the friendly kind that are usually encountered in America. They wore enormous sombreros and high-cut jackets with trousers that looked like gaiters. Their moustaches drooped and their eyes gleamed with mockery. They rode a mixed assortment of horses ranging from palominos to Arabs and some that were nondescript skewbalds. They carried rifles and bands of ammunition. The leader of the group grinned evilly, displaying teeth that had gold fillings. He spoke in the singsong manner of the English-speaking Mexican.

"Hey, Signors, you are lost ... I think. Do not worry, for a few dollars, we will take care of you."

As he spoke a couple of his companions started to open our bags and admire their contents.

He continued, "Come, we will take you to our encampment and make dealings with you."

They forced us at gun-point to mount two spare horses which were obviously intended as pack animals. They shared out our belongings and brought the bags along with them too as without speaking a word we had been engulfed in an even worse nightmare of a situation. They led our horses upon long lunges, which at least gave us the opportunity to quietly converse.

I said, "We are for it now, Holmes. They will rob us and then either kill us or just leave us to die in the desert."

To my surprise Holmes seemed somewhat unperturbed.

"Things are not quite as black as they appear, Watson. I believe that a rather surprising revelation is not far off."

I could not imagine what he meant, but I said nothing more for fear that these fierce desperados might shoot us on the slightest pretext. Eventually I saw in the distance a sort of encampment, with marquees and bell tents. I risked another comment to my friend, "We seem to have arrived at their bandit encampment."

He replied, "Rather sophisticated for a bandit's camp, don't you think, Watson? The marquee that we are making for must have cost many hundreds of dollars."

I dared one last comment, "Obviously crime pays well in these parts."

They made us dismount and then bundled us into the marquee, which had a canvas division within, so that we saw only about half of the inside. He who we had thought to be the leader announced that he would call his 'Beega boss', and he shouted something in what sounded like Spanish or the Mexican variation of it. In answer a really magnificent-looking fellow in a cloak, wearing a mask and a flat-topped hat of hard black felt, entered and stood hands on hips, gazing at us. He spoke in that which even I could detect to be a false Mexican accent.

He said, "Gentlemen, my men have found you and brought you here so that I will be forced to feed and house you. What will I get in return, surely not just these miserable articles of clothing?"

Then Holmes replied, and where I was amazed at his words, they brought forth a sudden change of manner in our captors. He said, "Well, Signor Zorro, I think the boot is on the other foot. You owe us food, drink and shelter in return for the inconvenience that you caused us when you bribed the guard to put us off the train in the middle of the desert. It is a good joke, but you really should not have spoiled it by wearing your Zorro costume ... Mr. Douglas Fairbanks!"

I was still bewildered, although the name Douglas Fairbanks rang an instant bell in my brain. I seemed to remember that he was a famous cinema actor, but I had never seen his films and would not have recognised him. Yet Sherlock Holmes had recognised him disguised by a mask and fancy costume. The actor threw back his head and laughed hugely, tearing away the domino mask and casting aside the hat.

He said, "I should myself have kept out of the way a little longer. I am flattered that you recognised me, Mr. Holmes."

My friend shrugged and explained.

"I seldom visit the cinema, yet I daily peruse a number of newspapers. About a year ago they almost all contained prominent advertising for a film titled *The Mark of Zorro* with photographic depictions of yourself in that costume complete with the mask. I may be retired, Mr. Fairbanks, but I have not lost my process of observation and memory."

Fairbanks nodded in comprehension.

"One forgets that being British does not mean that you live in a vacuum."

Holmes said, "Sir, you are sailing very close to impertinence to add to your rather unwelcome practical joke, which has engendered considerable discomfort for my colleague and myself. I demand now to be taken to my meeting with Charles Chaplin who will be anxious when we do not descend from the train at Los Angeles."

Fairbanks, obviously a man with a rather childlike side to his nature, almost collapsed with a fresh bout of laughter. When he could again speak clearly, he explained.

"He will certainly be surprised when he meets Sherlock Holmes and Dr. Watson in the persons of John Barrymore and Roland Young, who are currently engaged in those very roles in a film of your exploits."

I had no idea who Mr. Young was, let alone any idea of his appearance, but I had of course heard of John Barrymore and knew that he was a famous stage actor. As memory served me, Holmes had not been entirely displeased with William Gillette's portrayal of himself. But he was not delighted with the news.

"My dear Fairbanks … (He used the words so that the inference was not one of camaraderie) You stand there and add insult to injury. I feel that I could, given time, forgive your childish prank with the actors disguised as brigands, but to involve my client, Mr. Chaplin, for whom I have the greatest respect, in your schoolboy jape is quite unforgivable. I feel sure also that he will never forgive you."

The actor adopted a placating manner.

"My dear Mr. Holmes, I do apologise for any discomfort or annoyance that I may have caused you and your colleague. But you know Charlie would play a prank on me, just as daring if he could think it up. He and I are involved in a new company, United Artists and at the inaugural function he actually hired an actor to arrive disguised as a disreputable character, claiming to be my long-lost cousin. At another big function he got an actress to enter with a baby in a shawl, claiming that I was its father. This was done in front of my wife, Mary Pickford and all the Hollywood bigwigs. He deserves to be taken for a ride. But I admit that Dr. Watson and yourself have been unfortunate to get involved in my prank ... childish I suppose it is, and given time I will try to expunge it from your minds."

The canvas divider was drawn back and revealed comfortable chairs and all the trappings of civilised living. We were soon comfortably seated and plied with much needed refreshment, liquid and solid. I imagined Barrymore and Young, doubtless attired as we appeared in Paget's illustrations. I started to find it difficult not to chuckle at the thought of Chaplin's expression when he was close enough to realise what had been done.

I said, "No real harm done, Holmes, and I would love to see Chaplin's face when he discovered the substitution."

He grunted, but unwound enough to remark, "Well, if Chaplin can forgive it all, I suppose we can."

But he was still far from delighted.

The encampment turned out to be a location, as Fairbanks called it, for a film that the actor was making, titled *Son of Zorro* which explained the availability of the Mexican bandit costumes and horses. Indeed, Fairbanks allowed us to sit and watch several scenes being filmed, which for myself I found interesting. My mind was at rest with the promise that we would seen be conveyed to the hotel where Chaplin had arranged for us to reside.

"Camera, action!"

The director of the film shouted instructions through a megaphone and there was a whirring sound as the camera operator started his machine and Fairbanks, as Zorro attempted to leap up into the saddle of a horse. A formidable feat for any horseman, and the director made him repeat the action three times until he was happy with the scene. I was amazed at how much time and trouble was taken to capture on celluloid a movement which could scarcely occupy more than three or four seconds upon the screen. But if Fairbanks's superb athleticism was illustrated by this action, it was even more evident in another scene where he leapt from a moving horse onto a balcony where the heroine stood wringing her hands.

When Fairbanks joined us during a pause in his participation, I remarked to the effect that I had always believed that trained acrobats were substituted for the actors in such scenes. He assured me, "That is usually the case, Doctor, but I have always done my own stunts as we call them. I sustain injury now and again, but so far nothing serious."

At that point Holmes's keen eyes spotted a far distant vehicle at first just from its cloud of dust and soon after by the noise of an engine. He pointed it out to Fairbanks who was as surprised as anyone. Holmes explained,

"A model T Ford, followed by another vehicle which I believe is larger, like a truck or an ambulance."

This proved true and I was amazed at how Holmes could detect the differences of various motor engines. The model T stopped, driven by a man in a peaked cap and uniform of a policeman. Standing up in the back of the open topped car was another in a more ornate garb, evidently a high-ranking police officer. He had a large walrus moustache and beetling eyebrows. He shouted in a rasping voice,

"Which one of you is Douglas Fairbanks?"

Fairbanks stepped forward.

"The very same, Officer, what can I do for you?"

"I am here to arrest you for kidnapping and to take you to the county jail forthwith."

"Whom am I supposed to have kidnapped?"

"Two limeys called Jones and Watkins."

"You mean Holmes and Watson? Why, Officer, it was only a joke as they will tell you themselves."

He gestured at us. To my amazement Holmes said, "Ah, Captain, I am relieved to see you. We have been abducted and held prisoner by this person who is in fact impersonating a famous actor. I suggest you take him into custody at once."

The police captain (Holmes had evidently translated his rank from the insignia upon his uniform) flew into instant action, taking out a pair of handcuffs, which he locked upon Fairbanks's wrists. Then he blew a whistle and a door on the back of the second vehicle flew open and half a dozen men in police uniform tumbled out. There was something distinctly odd about them, for they were extremely ill-matched, with one of them extremely tall and thin, another incredibly stout and one with an unfortunate ocular condition which gave him permanently crossed eyes. They fell over each other in their efforts to reach and apprehend Fairbanks who by now was helpless with laughter.

He said, "I recognise Ben Turpin, Chester Conkin and the other Keystone Cops, but I don't know who you are, Captain. You play your part well."

Holmes smiled and said, "I recognised Mr. Chaplin as soon as he stepped down from the vehicle despite his excellent disguise. I do not believe that the American police would have enrolled a man of your, forgive me, diminutive height, Mr. Chaplin. Moreover, I recognised some English vowel sounds despite your well-disguised voice. You did not imagine that I would aid in your arrest had I not realised that it was a practical joke to match your own, my dear Fairbanks?"

Fairbanks laughed considerably and handed the disguised Chaplin the handcuffs.

"Here Charlie, you'd better take these!"

Chaplin started.

"How did you get out of those?"

There was a flash of white teeth beneath the hairline moustache as Fairbanks grinned hugely.

"I have many friends in this business, Charlie, including Harry Houdini."

*****

After we had been conveyed to the hotel and had a chance to wash and unpack, Chaplin sent a limousine to take us to his home in a superb area known as Beverley Hills. Before giving us dinner, he took us on the grand tour of the splendid house, which seemed to be a mixture of Victorian English and modern Spanish. It had upon the outside those terraces and conservatories that would have delighted Nash and even

Queen Victoria, yet inside it was airy and spacious with the cold stone floors of the Mediterranean. Evident in almost every room were depictions on canvas, in porcelain, plaster and even carved wood of the comic tramp that was the popular conception of our host the world over. He referred to these ever as 'The little fellow', as if divorcing himself from this persona.

As he showed us the master bedroom, Holmes enquired, "How long has Mrs. Chaplin been departed?"

Although I had seen no sign of Mrs. Chaplin, I failed to see why Holmes had not asked how long she had been away, instead of making it sound as if she had departed this Earth.

Chaplin smiled wryly.

"One Mrs. Chaplin has been gone for several months, another will arrive here within a few weeks as soon as the divorce is final. But how did you know that the departed one was not just away for the week, for there has as yet been no publicity."

Holmes explained.

"I knew that there had been a Mrs. Chaplin, but had suspected that you and she were estranged due to your complete failure to mention her to us at any time. This was confirmed by absence of one of a pair of framed portraits, presumably of you and your wife. Your portrait remains upon the wall, placed to balance with a scar upon the wall where her portrait hung."

I glanced at where Holmes pointed and noticed the very slightly lighter square, which matched Chaplin's portrait in size. "This often happens when a picture is taken from a wall to reveal a place where the decorations have been protected by the frame."

Chaplin nodded, understanding the deduction and saying,

"It is true the old Mrs. Chaplin has moved out and the new Mrs. Chaplin is just about to move in. It is a case of 'Off with the old and on with the new'; not unusual I might say in Beverley Hills."

Over a splendid dinner Holmes and I gave Chaplin a complete account of our activities since the last meeting we had experienced with him. He was, of course, disappointed that we had not the very best of news, but he was intrigued with that which we had discovered. He complimented Holmes upon his tenacity.

"You found out all that just by starting at the Austin's guesthouse. You see, I consider myself bright, yet I discovered absolutely nothing. My dear Holmes, when you tell me that you have failed, you forget that you have at least set my mind to some sort of rest. We now know that my mother is not only alive, but in greatly improved health, illustrated by these theatrical activities which you have discovered. I am delighted that she has retained her ability to entertain. She was always sad that she had nothing to give me, yet she gave me the most precious of gifts, a talent to amuse. I have inherited that talent from my dear mother, and I am now full of hope that you will eventually be able to find her. I assume you will try and pick up the trail again when you return to England?"

Holmes shook his head.

"No, I believe that she is in America now, possibly even in Hollywood itself."

"Good heavens, what makes you believe that?"

Chaplin seemed amazed, yet delighted. Holmes expanded upon the theme.

"The trail dried up at Southampton, and I believe that she had carefully planned to earn enough by that point to buy a steerage ticket to America."

He was excited. "But if what you believe is true, she must have been here for months, or rather more than a year. Yet she has not tried to contact me."

"In her own time, and in her own way, I believe she will. You see, I have formed the opinion that although she must know of your great success and affluence, the illness which plagued her mind is still there to the extent that she perhaps believes that all success is fleeting for that has been her own experience in life. She may also feel guilt for your unhappy childhood. Come, bizarre as it may sound, I believe that despite the passing of the years, she believes that she can make a career that will earn enough so that she can assist you if anything goes wrong with your career."

Chaplin whistled, "If you were not talking of my dear mother, it would sound bizarre; if it were any other one-time performer of her age. But I take the point of your words absolutely. Hannah and I were so close and I can only pray that we will be again."

Holmes leaned forward in his chair.

"We must now start to look for her among the people who are all but close to you. Remember, she has proved to be adept at disguise. Please study this photograph which I obtained from the photographer in Brighton."

Chaplin studied the middle-aged woman in the Pierrot dress and gasped.

"I can see that it is Mother, but only because I am looking for a likeness. But do you think her disguise will be even more thorough?"

Holmes nodded, "I think she will be feeling safe in that you will not recognise her."

For the rest of the evening Chaplin insisted upon entertaining us. When he was not playing the piano, singing or performing little pieces of what he called 'old vaudeville nonsense', he showed films for us in his own private cinema. He insisted upon accompanying these himself upon a second piano, which was there for that especial purpose, a small upright. The films were those that he had made during the previous two years when, he assured us, "I have at last had complete control over my work."

Sherlock Holmes watched these flickering screen plays with great attention and I noticed that his completely captured interest seemed to both please and greatly move our host.

Chapter Eight

'Walking into the Sunset'

On the day which followed we were taken to Chaplin's studio where he was shooting a film which he referred to as *A Day in the Park*, but which I believe eventually saw the light of day (or rather the dark of the cinema) under a completely different title. I got the impression that Mr. Chaplin had been working there for several hours before our arrival. It was somewhat different to the Fairbanks 'Zorro' experience, where the atmosphere had been a trifle free and easy. Here Mr. Chaplin was definitely in charge all the time, his directorial orders seeming strange to be emanating from 'The little tramp', as which he was attired.

But he received us kindly and seated us comfortably where we could observe everything without being intrusive.

One of Chaplin's assistants, a lady of some fifty-odd years tended to our requirements, bringing us tea, coffee and ice water in turns, even when we had no desire for it. She told us that her name was Thelma Morgan and that for the past two years she had been working for Charlie who she insisted was a firm, stern but a fair employer. She was an English woman so we had no language problems. It was hard not to notice that she had a rather scarred face, the result we were given to understand of a motor car accident. However, a liberal covering of heavy cosmetic make-up hid the worst of these lacerations. She was otherwise a bright and attractive woman with dark and flashing eyes.

Holmes asked her, "Miss Morgan, I wonder if I might ask for a list of the actors who are working in the production. It would save me from asking you 'Who is this?' or 'Who was that?' every few minutes?"

She provided, within minutes, a neatly typed list of players alongside the parts that they were playing.

It read as follows:

WORKING TITLE: A DAY IN THE PARK

The Little Fellow	Charles Chaplin
The Girl	Edna Purviance
Her Husband	Eric Campbell
The Park Keeper	Albert Austin
A Policeman	Oliver Hardy
2nd Policeman	Hilary Lyle
Girl's Mother	Athene Parsloe
Nursemaid	Zasu Pitts
Aunt Nellie	Connie Power
Uncle Harry	Edgar Kennedy
Apple Seller	Ann Richards
The Flirt	Lousie Fazenda
School Mistress	Marie Dressler

Whilst I did not know Holmes's particular reason for requesting this list I, of course, knew that to him every detail was important. But my attention I admit was diverted by what was happening around me. The Chaplin studio was smaller than I had imagined such places to be. In the centre of a quadrant of edifice (many of which I recognised from one of the films that I had seen in London), there was a square of artificial grass, bordered on one side by a path with a park bench and a lamp post. Further back, and evidently outside the range of the camera were a number of huge lamps, mounted upon tripods, each attended by a technician. The camera itself was on a wheeled trolley, which could be pushed forward or pulled backward by a number of workmen. As for

'Walking into the Sunset'

the cameraman, he was seated behind his camera, up on the trolley. He would peer through an appendage of the camera, rather like a pair of binoculars and when actually filming would turn a handle on the side of the instrument. Miss Morgan had evidently been delegated to explain all of this to us, otherwise the reader would not have received such a detailed account.

As for Chaplin, he was ever issuing orders to his cast and crew, and appeared to a casual observer even, such as myself, to be striving for absolute perfection in everything he controlled. There was for example a simple scene where the big policeman (Mr. Hardy) had simply to ogle the housemaid (Miss Pitts) and stroke his moustache as she pretended to ignore him, busying herself with a baby in a perambulator. The way these actors performed the actions looked perfectly fine to me the first time they did the scene. But Chaplin kept insisting that they do it again and again with changed emphasis.

"Babe, just touch your whiskers, don't tug them; and Zasu, darling, please make it clear that you are aware of him even whilst you are busy with the kid."

I suppose the scene was rehearsed a dozen times with various suggestions from Chaplin, but then to my surprise he had the actual scene filmed over and over again, breaking in with fresh instruction between each filming. I mentioned this, very quietly of course, to Miss Morgan, asking her, "Is it not rather expensive to film this one scene so many times?"

She nodded.

"Oh yes, and every scene in the film will be shot with the same determination for perfection. You see, Dr. Watson, when he worked for Mack Sennet everything was shot once, twice or at the very most three times. Sennet knew that he would make money with the pictures without there being any sort of perfection. Charlie always vowed that when he was his own master, his pictures would be absolutely perfect. I think perhaps he takes it a bit too far sometimes, but it is a good fault, is it not?"

I agreed, but Holmes, ever practical, asked,

"How can the expense be borne?"

She laughed.

"The film will cost many thousands of dollars to make, but it will yield many millions at the box office. Charlie felt that Sennet was just being greedy. (She lowered her voice.) They are both wrong in my opinion. Mack was too slapdash and Charlie is too meticulous. Somewhere in between would be right."

I noticed that Chaplin was just as strict with himself when he came into the next scene. All he had to do was to smile and tip his hat as he passed the girl (Miss Purviance) who was seated upon the bench. For the first actual take he shuffled past, pausing momentarily as he smiled engagingly and then raised his hat. She responded by turning her head away from him. I found this amusing to watch but evidently Chaplin was not happy with it. He repeated it, first raising the hat and then smiling more slowly. He waved his hands and shouted, "Cut! I believe I am being too obvious. Edna, try flashing your eyes at me first, then I will respond."

I will not bore the reader by listing all the possible ways that this simple scene could be played. Enough to say that Chaplin found at least twenty different ways before he was happy with it, and even then, he repeated it again and again.

To my surprise Holmes insisted upon attending several days of the filming, sitting alert yet silent as he observed everything. Of course, at first, I did not appreciate the system of filming, in so much as the scenes were not filmed in the order in which they would be shown. So, on our third day Chaplin took us into that section of his studio where the technical work was done. He explained how the scenes were numbered and filmed in an order convenient to the availability of settings.

He said, "What you saw yesterday and today all was centred upon that square of grass with the park bench. Now we have shot all of the park scenes no matter where in the film they will appear. Tomorrow we will be using the same space disguised as a street corner."

Holmes remarked, "I noticed that you filmed your scenes a great many times."

Chaplin replied, "I seek absolute perfection in my work, Mr. Holmes, just as you do in yours. I worked too long for those for whom anything would do if expense was spared to fall into that same trap myself. Let me show you how we assemble the film."

He threaded some of the film through an aperture which illuminated it, and enabled him to align one exposure with another, and so to join them through a complicated process of diagonal cutting and splicing with an acetone cement. I admit that I still preferred to retain the illusion that the cinema created, but Holmes was clearly fascinated with the information and remarked upon the small cuttings of film which lay around him upon the floor. When it was explained that these were wastage from the day's work, Holmes asked if he might keep a few of them. This made Chaplin chuckle and he collected a whole cardboard boxful of these short celluloid lengths. He presented these to my friend along with a small piece of equipment through which the pieces could be threaded and viewed by holding it up to the light. A tiny magnifier made viewing of the scrap of film quite easy.

He said, "A small souvenir of the Chaplin studio, eh, Holmes?"

Later, when I went to Holmes's room to remind him that it was time for dinner, I found him fully dressed for that occasion yet still too fascinated with his new toy to put it away. I noticed that he alternated his viewing of pieces of the film with a study of the list of actor's names which we had been given. He was engrossed and I had my work cut out to get him to join me in descending to the dining room.

Chaplin had another guest, a very famous actress, a Miss Pola Negri. When introduced to her I was surprised with her extreme normality, having long been used to depictions of her in character as 'the vamp'. But she was dressed in a very simple dark evening dress and there was no sign of the famous long cigarette holder.

"Mr Holmes, I have long had an ambition to appear in a film based upon one of your famous cases. But, alas, there are few solid roles for an actress save of the clinging vine variety."
It was Chaplin who answered her.
"What about *A Scandal in Bohemia*?"
But it was left to Holmes to give this the thumbs down.
"Miss Negri would be quite miscast as Irene Adler."
He spoke a little sharply and I fancied he ruffled her feathers a trifle. She said, "One got the impression from your friend's account of the episode that you were somewhat enamoured with Miss Adler?"
Holmes's turn it was to snap,
"I admired her mind, Miss Negri, something which I cannot say I have experienced with a member of the female sex before. I always think of Miss Adler as 'the woman'."
Pola Negri pushed her plate from her and said, "Well, that is me put in my place, eh, Charlie?"
Chaplin reduced the tension, chuckling as he said, "How would it be if we made a version of *The Hound of the Baskervilles* starring Rin Tin Tin?"
She tried not to smile, and then said, "That lets me out; Miss Stapleton is an ingénue."
Chaplin replied, "But you have forgotten the other female role, Mrs. Barrymore. I can just picture you, Pola, signalling through the window with an oil lamp to the convict on the moors."
At this she was forced to laugh, "What will you play, Charlie?"
He became almost surreal. "Why Dr. Watson, of course."
Even Holmes entered into the spirit of this ironic casting.
"No doubt you have an actor in mind to play myself other than Gillette or John Barrymore?"
Chaplin could scarcely speak for laughing as he suggested, "How about Babe Hardy?"
Holmes joined in the general laughter that ensued, at the thought of the heavily built actor with the huge round red face playing the great detective. We were aware that he played one of the two policemen in the film that Chaplin was currently

making, the two actors obviously having been chosen for the roles that they might contrast with each other in height, build and style.

Over the dessert Holmes took the opportunity to enquire concerning one or two other members of Chaplin's cast.

"Miss Purviance and Marie Dressler are familiar to me by name as established players, but I do not believe I have come to hear as yet of Miss Fazenda, or Miss Parsloe. I noticed that the last named appears heavily veiled at all times."

Pola Negri said, "I have had Athene Parsloe in several of my films. A real old battle axe. But Louise Fazenda is very easy to work with, and a very funny woman."

Chaplin continued, "I am lucky that she was available, she plays the flirt to perfection. I have worked with most of the rest of he cast before. Why Eric Campbell and Albert Austin are practically members of my family. Zasu Pitts is a joy to work with. I had never encountered Ann Richards or Connie Power before, but they have both turned out well. You know Annie plays the apple seller, not a big part, but the scene where I steal the apple to give to the girl depends on Annie's reaction, which was perfect. Connie Power is so muffled up as Aunt Nellie that it is difficult to assess her potential, but she works like a professional."

It was clear to me that Holmes was seeking information but had disguised the enquiries as small talk, rather well I felt. I understood his train of thought in seeking information regarding those actresses who were heavily disguised, elderly, and little known. The thought that Hannah Chaplin might be right under our noses and actually working for her son was a daring one that had not occurred to me but obviously it had to my friend.

After dinner was over Chaplin entertained us by showing a new film of his, which had not as yet been shown at the picture houses, in his own private cinema. It was a fine film, charming, amusing, and yet tugging at the heartstrings. It concerned an itinerant workman who befriends a homeless orphan, played by a child actor, Jackie Coogan. I was reduced to helpless laughter when the child broke windows so that his benefactor could gain employment as a glazier, making the repairs. I noticed that Chaplin and Pola Negri seemed very close in their friendship as they sat holding hands in the dark like a young couple at the cinema. When it was over and lights went up, she threw her arms round him and exclaimed, "Wonderful, Charlie ... you've done it again!"

We also congratulated our host, for it was not difficult to recognise a work of cinematic genius, such as we had seen, even with as little knowledge of the cinema as my own.

After Pola Negri had departed in her Rolls Royce, Chaplin joined us for a final smoke and cup of coffee. We discussed the film that we had seen, the film he was making and our preoccupation with Hannah Chaplin, her safety, welfare and whereabouts. But I do not believe that Chaplin connected this conversation with Holmes's request which followed it.

My friend asked, "Do you think it would be possible for me to appear in one of the scenes in your film?"

I was as amazed as Chaplin clearly was. His reply held a mixture of embarrassment and bewilderment.

"Why, I guess I could work you into a scene, but I will have to give the matter some thought. Do you have a special reason for wishing to do so?"

Holmes explained, "Yes. I thought it might be rather amusing for you to be able to show the film to friend Fairbanks and ask him to try and spot which of the actors was Sherlock Holmes. I would be heavily disguised of course. I could become one of your crowd players for a day."

Chaplin's face relaxed into a broad grin.

"What a splendid gag! Why, yes, it would be easy to work you in. Forgive my reticence when I had thought you were after some sort of leading role."

After Chaplin had retired, Holmes explained to me the real purpose of his planned escapade.

"I am not screen struck, Watson. I wish to mingle with the small-part players in the faint possibility that Hannah Chaplin is among them. Two or three of the ladies discussed tonight interest me as possibilities, but were I to attempt some direct open interrogation, I fear I might scare our quarry."

'Walking into the Sunset'

I understood, yet there was an aspect of it that I wondered if he had overlooked.

"But, Holmes, it is possible that Hannah, if she is among the cast as you suspect, may have her own plans regarding the moment of revelation. Perhaps you might spoil her big moment?"

"I understand your thought, Watson, but the fact remains that I have been engaged to find her. Moreover, the lady has been disturbed in her mind and might lurk unrecognised forever without intending to reveal herself. I think we owe it to Charles and Hannah to bring about their reunion for both of their sakes. To put his mind at rest and to ensure that her future is secure."

He was right, of course, for Hannah might well even decide to disappear from the scene once she had become assured that Charlie was indeed established and happy. She might wish never to make herself known to him for fear that embarrassment could result, little knowing the joy that the reunion would bring him. But, of course, it was also in my mind that Hannah was not even within a hundred miles of the studio, content to observe Charlie from afar – and possibly from a position of poverty. Holmes was right, the mother and her son deserved to be reunited.

When I came to the breakfast table on the morning following, I was surprised to find that Holmes was absent from it, for he invariably took his place before I occupied my own. I enquired of the butler, "Have you seen Mr. Holmes today?"

He replied, "No, sir, but I understand from Mr. Chaplin that he left the house at a very early hour."

I looked into Holmes's room hoping to gain some clue and saw his make-up box upon the dressing table. Of course! I had forgotten that the crowd players arrived at the studio at about five-thirty in the morning, and Holmes would have needed to attend to his disguise.

When later a car took me to the studio, I found it very difficult to spot Holmes among the roughly dressed loungers who stood upon the mock street corner that had been erected. I tried to apply the science of deduction in recognising my friend among so many nondescripts. I considered first the question of height. There were of the twenty or so involved only half a dozen who were tall enough to be Sherlock Holmes. Of these three were far too heavily built to be him, even allowing for their possibly padded state. Of the three that remained, two appeared as clean-shaven and with noses that were far too small. (One can disguise the nasal appendage with putty, but this will only add to its size.) The lounger with the battered hat, large nose and moustache, therefore, must be my friend. I noted that he wisely kept well to the background as the comic ballet of characters unfolded. Chaplin, evidently holding back his own participation until a later stage sat in his directorial chair, wearing his shabby tramp suit and the pale make-up with the small moustache for which he was so well known. His bowler hat lay beside him upon the ground, leaving his luxuriant dark hair to tumble where it would. The serious and rapt expression upon his face so contrasted with 'the little fellow', the character around which the whole film revolved. But here that comic axis had become for the moment a calculating observer with all the responsibility imaginable upon his rounded shoulders. He rapped out orders, cajoling, bullying, coaxing, in turns to extract the very finest from his company.

"Annie, don't forget you think you are Pavlova. Athene, get up on your toes, try at least! Excellent, Babe, keep that up; you, too, Hilary – in your minds you are a couple of cops who want to be dancers."

The two matronly women and the two comic policemen made an amusing centrepiece with Babe Hardy surprisingly light on his feet despite his two hundred and fifty pounds, and Hilary Lyle, a little fellow who made such a contrast, and I could predict in my mind that the two of them would make an excellent comedy team with a big future. Ann Richards had a comic brilliance, too, as she tried to get up onto points which could surely only have been the result of many years of vaudeville experience. The same could be said for Athene Parsloe. I marvelled at the endurance of all these comic dancers, keeping up their balletic movements for so long as Chaplin made them repeat each sequence over and over again.

I could see that Holmes was taking advantage of this opportunity to study both principals and his fellow crowd players. Then when it was time for Chaplin himself to participate, he dismissed the crowd people and he and Edna Purviance became the centrepiece of the balletic satire. I was amazed at what a fine dancer he proved to be. Of course, he was comical with his steps, but it takes an expert to burlesque effectively. Shakespeare was so right when he said, 'It takes a wise man to be a fool'. Charlie Chaplin was a wise man and a sublime fool, and was as relentless with his own work as he had been with the others.

As for Holmes, I noted that he had retreated to a dressing tent with the other supernumeraries. I was not to see him again until we met at Chaplin's dinner table that evening.

As we dined, I was struck by the amazing vitality of Charlie Chaplin as he worked hard to keep us entertained with well-honed anecdotes and pleasing foolery with the forks, spoons and plates. He could juggle like an expert and balance upon his hands like an acrobat with no signs of the hard day's work even slowing him down. This time there were no other guests, but he explained the reason for this.

"Tomorrow is the last day of shooting, and there are only a few short scenes involved. But tomorrow night we will have a party with all of the cast and workers invited."

I had noticed that Holmes was preoccupied, having written the name Lily Harley upon a note pad. Whilst Chaplin could not see what he was writing, he was aware of Holmes's preoccupation and said, "My dear Holmes, perhaps I have bored you with my distraction and maybe you want me to enter some serious discussion concerning your ruse of masquerading as a crowd player for me this day?"

Holmes smiled and said politely, "You, sir, could never bore me, but I admit to a certain amount of preoccupation connected with my day as a film extra. I will not raise false hopes, my dear Chaplin, but I feel secure in saying that I may be able to make some sort of disclosure to you by this time tomorrow evening."

The little comedy genius was alert as he said, "I will not press you for clues, Holmes, because I know that anything you have to tell me you will do when the time is right for you to do so. Now, gentlemen, although you might not believe it, I am really very tired and I think I will turn in early tonight. Pray do not hesitate to call upon my staff who will, I know, see to your every need."

I could well believe that Chaplin was really tired despite the impression of vitality that he had given at the dinner table. He was a consummate professional, able to cover his fatigue with the clown's mask. We both thanked him and wished him a pleasant rest. After he had left us, I asked my friend,

"It is true then that you really have made progress?"

"Yes, Watson, I believe I have. You see everything has fallen into place in my mind. But I am desperate not to make any error which would leave our host heartbroken. I must tread softly, yet I feel that tomorrow evening is the time for me to lay cards upon the table and chance my arm."

When I rang for the butler, to my surprise it was Thelma Morgan who answered that ring. She explained to us, "The butler is busy making preparation for tomorrow night, but I thought I would myself answer your bell rather than send you a maid."

In the bright artificial light, her heavy make-up looked even more theatrical than when we had seen her in daylight. She was also somewhat muffled up with a tasteful silk scarf around her neck. She said she would bring the pot of coffee which we had requested, and when she had left the room, Holmes remarked, "I believe there are staff enough to have waited upon us without the need for Chaplin's secretary to need to serve us."

"You mean she may feel some need to impart some information to us?"

"Possibly, Watson, but, in any case, I feel sure she will reveal her interest in us shortly."

'Walking into the Sunset'

When she returned with the coffee pot she said, "Mr Holmes, I believe for many years you had a landlady, a Mrs. Hudson?"

Holmes replied, "That is so, Miss Morgan. Why do you ask?"

"Oh, I just wondered if she owned the house at 221B Baker Street, or did you merely employ her?"

It was my turn to answer.

"The house belonged to the good lady and her husband, Miss Morgan. When Holmes and I took the rooms, our payment was to include her service and that of a pageboy."

She said, surprisingly, "Ah yes, Billy. I have read many of your accounts of your friend's exploits, Doctor, but was not quite sure about Mrs. Hudson. Well, gentlemen, if you need anything else please do not hesitate to ring."

She wished us goodnight and departed, but did not curtsey as a maid would have done. I felt that she was decidedly odd and remarked as much to my friend. But Holmes merely shrugged and said, "Many people are odd, Watson, some because they are born that way, and others simply appear odd through strange behaviour which eventually becomes explained. You will soon know which form of oddness is enjoyed by Miss Thelma Morgan."

*****

Charlie Chaplin's party for the cast was indeed a glittering affair. A wonderful buffet dinner was followed by a modern dance band and Chaplin treated us to a wonderful burlesque Apache dance which he performed with Louise Fazenda. It was obvious to everyone that it had been well rehearsed, yet another tribute to his stamina and professionalism.

Then during what some would refer to as 'the shank of the evening' when all save cast principals and Chaplin's personal friends had departed, we were gathered in a circle for a nightcap. Sherlock Holmes quite suddenly made a somewhat startling announcement. His words obviously surprised

Chaplin as much as anyone and he leant forward attentively as Holmes spoke.

"Ladies and gentlemen, as most of you are aware by now my name is Sherlock Holmes, but as you may not know, I have been engaged by Mr. Chaplin in the task of trying to discover where his mother, Hannah, might be. Contact between them was lost in a manner which I would prefer to keep confidential, as it no longer affects my quest. After many enquiries, I managed to establish that Mrs. Chaplin had, despite advancing years, returned to the theatrical profession using a new *nom de théâtre* and evidently with some modest success. She had, I felt sure, eventually left Great Britain from Southampton and arrived in America, the better part of two years ago."

Holmes paused and asked if he might have some black coffee, which was quickly found for him. There was no buzz of conversation during the moments when he sampled the coffee and collected himself to deliver the rest of his speech. There was a silence during which a pin could have been heard, should anyone have been unwise enough to drop one.

He continued, "My investigations concerning Mrs. Hannah Chaplin had led me to believe that she would want to be near to her son to assure herself of his well being and yet wish as yet to keep her own counsel. With her discovery that her histrionic talent had survived many years of non use, it was natural that she would want to gain a role in one of her son's films. Of course, many people have tried without success to do the same. Miss Morgan, I believe you auditioned for parts in Mr. Chaplin's films before settling for the less spectacular but more reliable role of a secretary?"

Thelma Morgan was a little taken aback, but recovered her composure quickly, saying, "Is it not a pleasure to serve Mr. Chaplin in any capacity?"

Holmes nodded and then said, "The lady I searched for was perhaps some fifty-five or six years of age, but from my enquiries in Britain it was obvious that she had a vitality and quality of performance that would pass for those of a younger woman. Now Chaplin had not seen his mother in many years, but obviously he would recognise her without some form of disguise. There were three actresses in the film that has just been completed who from the point of view of age, would fit my quest.

"Miss Parsloe, for example, but this lady's height immediately eliminated her as a possibility. Miss Power was nearer to Hannah in that respect, but the colouration of the eyes, which are almost impossible to disguise, and other minor differences (which I noticed only when posing as a screen extra) eliminated her also. I was left with Miss Richards as the only possibility among the female principals. For a while I felt that muffled up as she was in her role of the apple seller, I could have found the woman I was seeking. But in the street corner scene in which I participated I was close enough to the lady to perceive that she was wearing a glove upon her right hand with two padded fingers, indicating that the real fingers had been lost. Unless this had happened very recently, this would discount Miss Richards entirely."

At this point Ann Richards, almost unrecognisable as the old apple lady in a svelte evening dress, stood up and removed the black gloves which she was wearing to reveal the missing first and second fingers of her right hand. We could all see the well-advanced signs of the healing process. As a medical man I felt that I should step forward and make an examination, which I did, very quickly remarking, "The injuries are at least ten years old, Holmes."

Ann Richards started to replace her gloves as she said, "About twelve years ago actually, Doctor. I was doing a scene in a Keystone comedy which involved a tame lion, but he turned out to be a little less tame than was claimed."

Chaplin broke in to ask, "So, your disguise in the park scene did not reveal anyone among the extras who might have been a suspect, if I can refer to my own dear mother as such?"

My friend responded, "You will have seen for yourself through their presence at this function a little earlier that most of the female supernumeraries were too young to be considered."

Sherlock Holmes and the Charlie Chaplin Affair

Charles Chaplin shrugged, and said, "Mr. Holmes, I do not quite understand. From what you have told us your enquiries seem to have had little success, and yet you had intimated otherwise."

When Sherlock Holmes replied to Chaplin, he took on the manner of an actor manager making a curtain speech. This final oration was dynamic and revelatory.

"What I have told you is accurate, yet my quest has not been in vain. At the first day of my observation of the filming, I requested and was given a list of the cast members and the parts that they played. This was, of course, useful to me if only for purposes of elimination. But it was only when despairing of success that I studied the names. I did this not with any thought of making any great discovery, rather from a desire to explore every possible avenue. Watson will tell you that I have long been fascinated with words, conundrums and anagrams. I examined the cast list with this aspect in mind. When a person wishes to take on a fresh persona, they often rearrange the letters of their name and produce a new one in this way. Usually they are unable to produce a perfect anagram, but will be happy with something that is close. Where this has happened, one can sense the possibility of coincidence but the perfect anagram is not usually coincidental. There was upon that list a name which was the perfect rearrangement of the name used by the lady I was seeking."

Chaplin interrupted at this point and demanded that Miss Morgan bring him the cast list, which she was able to do with her usual rapid competence. He scanned it quickly. Although largely self-educated, I knew that he was a shrewd man and would soon spot something like an anagram. He lowered the paper and said, "Holmes, there is no woman's name on this list that is an anagram of Hannah Chaplin."

Holmes replied gently, "Your mother used another name in her earlier professional days, did she not?"

"Yes, she was known as Lily Harley, but at a glance I can see that this name is no possibility either."

My friend took the list from Chaplin and taking a pencil from his inside dress coat pocket he circled one of the names and returned the list to the comedian. Chaplin gazed in disbelief at what he saw.

"Holmes, you are jesting and I consider it to be a pretty poor sort of joke, if I might say so. I can see, of course, that the name Hilary Lyle is indeed a perfect anagram of Lily Harley, but this must surely be some sort of once in a lifetime bizarre coincidence? Mr. Lyle is a valued member of the cast, responding so well to my direction. He is obviously an artiste of great experience and I feel sure would not wish to trick me in any way."

Amazed as any other I watched as Hilary Lyle, a small figure in a rather over-large dress suit, tugged at his grey moustache and appeared to be anxious to leave the gathering. Holmes crossed over to him and dropped a hand upon his shoulder. Again, to my amazement he said, "Mrs. Chaplin, in your efforts to assist your son and desire not to embarrass him you have gone a little bit too far. Your disguise is perfect as I would expect from a consummate artiste. Your son longs to have you back as his beloved mother. Please give him the greatest gift you can."

Charles Chaplin stood in frozen disbelief as Hilary Lyle removed the false grey whiskers and smiled in winsome fashion. It was indeed Hannah Chaplin who stood before us all.

Then at length she spoke. "Darling Charlie, my deception was for two ends: the first that I might work for you and make up for some of the deprivation that you suffered while I was caring for you. The second, I thought perhaps that if I could prove myself capable still of earning a living as an artiste, there would never be any chance of my being put into an asylum again."

Within seconds mother and son were in each other's arms and both were sobbing with joy and emotion. Everyone else present preserved a silence born of amazement at the scene which had unfolded before them. At length Miss Morgan took Hannah upstairs to find her some more suitable clothing.

Sherlock Holmes and the Charlie Chaplin Affair

During the minutes that they were absent, Chaplin tried to embrace Sherlock Holmes who backed away with embarrassment.

"My dear Holmes, I cannot thank you enough. You have made this a party that I will always remember. You have bewildered and astounded me in turns, and finally delighted me beyond all expectations. Dear Mother, the word asylum shall never be mentioned again in her hearing. I have for some time had a beautiful home for her which was constructed especially. It even has a tiny theatre built into it and I shall provide her with a companion who will manage everything and take all worries from her mind. I will visit her every day and will be able to take her to theatres and to restaurants. She will enjoy all those things that cruel fate has denied her."

When Hannah reappeared on Thelma's arm, she was clad in a fine evening dress produced from I know not where. Thelma had also provided her with cosmetics, which between them they had used to transform an elderly balletic comedian into a beautiful woman, radiant through joy and relief. The band had long departed but Chaplin played phonograph discs and the dancing and merry making went on until the dawn.

Everyone hugged Hannah before they departed and we stayed long enough with Charlie Chaplin to enjoy visiting Hannah in her splendid new home. My last sight of her was when on her son's arm, she retreated into the sunset, the scene being just like that which ended so many of Chaplin's screen plays. Usually it was the heroine of the picture that was on his arm; yet Hannah Chaplin, or Lily Harley was a real-life heroine rather than a figure on flickering celluloid.

"With five volumes you could fill that gap on that second shelf."
(Sherlock Holmes, *The Empty House*)

So why not complete your collection of murder mysteries from Baker Street Studios? Available from all good bookshops, or direct from the publisher with free UK postage & packing. To see full details of all our publications, range of audio books, and special offers visit www.crime4u.com where you can also join our mailing list.

IN THE DEAD OF WINTER
MYSTERY OF A HANSOM CAB
SHERLOCK HOLMES AND THE ABBEY SCHOOL MYSTERY
SHERLOCK HOLMES AND THE ADLER PAPERS
SHERLOCK HOLMES AND THE BAKER STREET DOZEN
SHERLOCK HOLMES AND THE BOULEVARD ASSASSIN
SHERLOCK HOLMES AND THE CHINESE JUNK AFFAIR
SHERLOCK HOLMES AND THE CHILFORD RIPPER
SHERLOCK HOLMES AND THE CIRCUS OF FEAR
SHERLOCK HOLMES AND THE DISAPPEARING PRINCE
SHERLOCK HOLMES AND THE DISGRACED INSPECTOR
SHERLOCK HOLMES AND THE EGYPTIAN HALL ADVENTURE
SHERLOCK HOLMES AND THE FRIGHTENED GOLFER
SHERLOCK HOLMES AND THE GIANT'S HAND
SHERLOCK HOLMES AND THE GREYFRIARS SCHOOL MYSTERY
SHERLOCK HOLMES AND THE HAMMERFORD WILL
SHERLOCK HOLMES AND THE HILLDROP CRESCENT MYSTERY
SHERLOCK HOLMES AND THE HOLBORN EMPORIUM
SHERLOCK HOLMES AND THE HOUDINI BIRTHRIGHT
SHERLOCK HOLMES AND THE LONG ACRE VAMPIRE
SHERLOCK HOLMES AND THE MAN WHO LOST HIMSELF
SHERLOCK HOLMES AND THE MORPHINE GAMBIT
SHERLOCK HOLMES AND THE SANDRINGHAM HOUSE MYSTERY
SHERLOCK HOLMES AND THE SECRET MISSION
SHERLOCK HOLMES AND THE SECRET SEVEN
SHERLOCK HOLMES AND THE TANDRIDGE HALL MURDER
SHERLOCK HOLMES AND THE TELEPHONE MURDER MYSTERY
SHERLOCK HOLMES AND THE THEATRE OF DEATH
SHERLOCK HOLMES AND THE THREE POISONED PAWNS
SHERLOCK HOLMES AND THE TITANIC TRAGEDY
SHERLOCK HOLMES AND THE TOMB OF TERROR
SHERLOCK HOLMES AND THE YULE-TIDE MYSTERY
SHERLOCK HOLMES: A DUEL WITH THE DEVIL
SHERLOCK HOLMES AT THE RAFFLES HOTEL
SHERLOCK HOLMES AT THE VARIETIES
SHERLOCK HOLMES ON THE WESTERN FRONT
SHERLOCK HOLMES: THE GHOST OF BAKER STREET
SPECIAL COMMISSION
THE ADVENTURE OF THE SPANISH DRUMS
THE CASE OF THE MISSING STRADIVARIUS
THE ELEMENTARY CASES OF SHERLOCK HOLMES
THE TORMENT OF SHERLOCK HOLMES
THE TRAVELS OF SHERLOCK HOLMES
WATSON'S LAST CASE

Baker Street Studios Limited, Endeavour House, 170 Woodland Road, Sawston, Cambridge CB22 3DX
sales@baker-street-studios.com

Lightning Source UK Ltd.
Milton Keynes UK
UKHW020646170822
407432UK00010B/1365